Dedication

This piece is dedicated to those who have supported me in my journeys; whether it's been since the beginning of time, or whether the supporters are new, with my station! This includes all of my family, my circle of friends, and all of my teachers who have helped with my studies, and those teachers who have also helped in developing my writing skills.

I can't forget to let you know, that this book is dedicated to YOU. Without you, what would I be but a mere citizen with a dream? Your continued support is what keeps me going forward; I guarantee, I will not let you down!

I would like to give a special shoutout to those who helped me piece together and edit this work; your efforts are not going unnoticed.

As you read this new piece, I ask that you read it, as though you've never known who B.M. Gage is; as though you've never heard my voice before; as though you've never listened to my show and have NO IDEA how I think. Read it with a new mind; if you don't know who I am, that's even better! All I ask is that you learn more about me by listening to my show on The Heat, https://theheatdb.com, and following my Facebook page (facebook.com/officialbmgage) and my Twitter (twitter.com/officialbmgage).

1

It was a cold Saturday morning when I awoke. In my pool of sweat, I swam to the other side of the bed to shut off my alarm clock. With each stroke, my slight headache became unbearable; its slow throbbing was reminiscent of a heavy door being slammed shut. The alarm clock joined in on the madness; its obnoxious buzzing transforming my head into a bomb due to explode at any minute. Interestingly enough, my heart was left out in all the commotion. It decided to speed up its rate until I was breathless as well frighten at the idea of it bursting out my chest. Finally, I reached shore and turned off my alarm.

Did I party too hard last night?

Gathering strength, I got out of bed and walked to the bathroom. I scanned it for a moment before entering.

Copyright Notice

Author's Note

Here we are, 3 releases later. It's been an interesting journey, to say the least, but I've managed to get it done. As you jump into my fourth work, I hope that you all enjoy this work from start to finish.

I decided that you needed the full story. *Flirting With Death* jumps directly into the action with Richard, Jared, Linda, and Julie, but you never really found out how it all began. When writing *The Sixth Sense*, I decided to take it back so that you could develop and grow with the characters. After reading this work, I want for you to be able to understand why things went down the way they did in the later works. Your questions shall be answered.

Be YOU-tiful and enjoy my latest piece. As always, I value all feedback; https://facebook.com/officialbmgage. Thank you!

Remember; don't let anyone tell you what you can't do! Do you, because only you can do you the way that you do, you…

The bathroom's still neat, so last night couldn't have been that bad.

After using the lavatory, I turned on the sink. I closed my eyes and let my hands float in the pool of warm water. Minus the challenge of waking up, I felt out of sync this morning. Physically, I was present, but something pulled me in a different state mentally. I couldn't pin down what exactly caused this; I just knew I didn't wake up as my ordinary self. Opening my eyes, I looked at myself in the mirror before splashing water in my face. As the water dripped from my jawbones, I saw a mental image of a black van smashing through the glass of a bank and running through red lights.

What the hell?

I tightened the water faucet and headed into the living room. I grabbed my cellphone from the coffee table, checking if I received any new assignments to perform for the day. While scrolling, I plopped onto the couch and turned on the television.

"In developing news, police are examining a bank subjected to an early morning robbery. On your screen is security footage of two robbers bursting through the rear of Ester Communion Bank with roughly two million dollars. We hand it over to Tanya Phillips, live from Ester Communion Bank as the story unfolds."

I'm losing it. I'd just seen this incident play out in my mind. From the car to the bank. What the fuck is going on? Alright, just calm down. Maybe it was just a coincidence. Just prepare for the day.

I turned off the TV and made my way back to the bathroom, hoping I didn't have any visions again. After a long, hot shower, I got dressed. Suddenly, my phone rang. It was Linda.

Clearing my throat, I answered, "good morning, Linda."
"Hey, Richard," Linda replied. "Did you by chance see the news this morning? There was a robbery—"
I interrupted, "at Ester Communion Bank by two masked robbers driving off in a Chevrolet Black suburban. Yeah, I saw it."

Linda chuckled, "No crime goes unnoticed on your watch, Detective."

I snickered back, "Yeah, something like that. Look, I'm gonna swing by there before heading to the station. Wait for me; I wanna talk to you about something."

"Okay, well, I'll wait for a little while," Linda said. "If you take more than twenty minutes, I'm leaving. I can't risk getting fired."

"I'll be there in five," I joked. "We won't get fired. But I do think you want to hear this."

"Alright, Rick. See you in a few."

I hung up the phone as I walked out the door. I got in the car, waited for it to warm up, and drove over to Linda's. I couldn't help but mentally replay everything that happened to me this morning: the challenging aspect of getting out of bed; the vision in the bathroom; the breaking news. What did all of this mean? I wanted to spend more time thinking over these puzzling events, but I arrived at Linda's. I exited the vehicle, ensured it was locked and walked towards her porch. Linda opened the door before I even got to the doorstep.

"You're late," Linda stated as she looked at her phone. "I was expecting you 30 seconds ago."

"Yeah, well, you know, traffic," I replied. "You gonna let me in? It's cold out here."

Pointing at me, Linda replied, "I should let you stand out here and freeze to death. Come in."

As I walked inside, Linda closed the door and headed to the back. I made my way to her couch and slumped down on it. My headache came back with a mild vengeance. Though less violent as the former, I found myself laying down on the couch cradling my head wishing the pain stopped. Linda returned with two cups of coffee and a concerned look when seeing my disposition.

"You okay?" She asked.

"Yeah, I'm fine," I said as I sat up. "Did you enjoy yourself last night at the banquet?"

She replied while handing me one of the cups, "it was nice conversing with old classmates and former coworkers. How did you feel about it?"

"I think I may have overdone it last night," I stated as I thought about the vision from earlier.

"You don't say," Linda said.

I took a sip of the coffee and rose to my feet. I paced the floor.

"Remember I told you I had something to tell you."

"Yes," Linda answered.

I thought of how to word it.

"I woke up to a terrible headache and a racing heart. When I finally got out of bed to wash my face, I envisioned a getaway van crashing through the doors of Ester Communion Bank."

Linda looked at me with a concerned expression.

"You think I'm crazy, huh?" I asked her.

"Not quite. I've heard of this happening to people. I see it on television all the time," she replied.

I stopped pacing and looked at her.

"This is real life, Linda. I'm not joking. It's like I can see into the future."

Linda began, "maybe it was just a case of déjà vu. You know..."

As Linda spoke, my mind faded from reality and showed me another vision. I now saw the two fugitives from the bank parking at a home. I got a view of the address: 2634 S. Banks Ave.

I faded back into reality; Linda knew I hadn't been paying attention.

"Did you hear a word I just said?" she chuckled.

"It just happened again," I spoke. "The two fugitives at the address 2634 S. Banks. What they were doing, I don't know," I sat back down in the chair.

"Damn, Rick, you keep this up, you're going to make all of us look bad at the station," Linda joked. "I think you have been given the gift of the sixth sense." She set her cup down on the table. "Do you think we should head over there?"

"No," I said, "I say we head to the station for now and see what's going on. There may be updates that we need in to follow this case."

"I'm fine by that order," Linda spoke.

We each put on our coats and left the house and drove to the police station.

"Can't wait until the weather warms up," I said as I got out of the vehicle and rubbed my hands together.

"Don't forget, this is Chicago... it's 40 today, but could be 80 tomorrow." Linda chuckled as we walked inside.

"Detective Young, Officer Jackson," the woman at the front desk stated when she saw Linda and me.

"Morning, Isabella," I said.

"Abel has been looking all over for both of you. I know you both heard about this morning's bank robbery."

"I take it, that's the case we are assigned to," I spoke as I looked through the mail in my slot.

"Exactly," Isabella spoke. "They're having a meeting in the conference room, so head on back there."

Linda and I walked into the conference room.

"Young, Jackson, so glad that you could join us," Abel spoke.

"Sorry we're late," I stated as I sat down.

"Now we can get things started. I assume each of you has heard about the robbery this morning."

"The fugitives came speeding down my block this morning," Linda said. "I couldn't be 100% certain at the time, but now, I'm positive it was them."

Abel continued to speak.

"And you all should know, they got away with over two million."

"Damn; why didn't we just take that shit?" a male officer chuckled.

"Jared, maybe it's because we work for the right team," I laughed lightly.

"I know if I had that kind of money, I definitely wouldn't be in Chicago right now," Jared joked.

Abel interrupted, "and might I add that you two jackasses would be facing up to fifteen years minimum for breaking the law, simply for the fact that you're an enforcer of the law."

Jared and I looked down in silence.

Abel pressed the button on the remote in his hand and the projector turned on. It displayed a driver's license and a black suburban.

"Now, we ran the license plate of the getaway vehicle, and it's registered to a 'James Kingston'. Kingston is deceased, and the plate is registered to a completely different vehicle. So, we have what we believe is a stolen plate. All we have at this point is an address on the license plate. However, since it isn't correct, we are kind of at a stand-still."

"So, we're gonna start at the crime scene," I said.

"Correct," Abel replied.

"Do you think we have any leads? Are there any potential suspects?" Jared asked.

"We can't be 100% sure," he moved to the next screen, "but we have our eye on one suspect; her name is Julie Wilson. No prior arrests or convictions, but she has had quite a few run-ins with the law. Speeding tickets up the ass, and during one traffic stop, an officer spoke of seeing some kind of blueprint of a bank in her car. When he asked her about it, she said she was a contractor, and showed him a valid contractor's license."

I looked at the woman.

"This is the woman you're thinking did this?" I asked. "She doesn't even look capable of doing something like this."

"I would think you'd know by now that looks can be deceiving, Detective," Abel replied. "Back in school, teachers had to call the police many times because of Wilson's science fair projects. She designed a cherry bomb at the age of 11."

"So, where does she live?" Jared asked.

"She lives in the Flossmoor area. 2634 S. Banks. Can't miss it; damn near a mansion."

The address... it was the address I'd previously seen while I was talking to Linda.

"In the meantime, Richard, Linda, Jared, and Madeline: I'm sending you all out to the crime scene to look at the evidence. View the security tapes, dust for prints, do whatever you have to do. We cannot let these pieces of shit stay on our streets."

Isabella walked into the room. "I'm sorry to interrupt but sending any officers to the crime scene for evidence would be a waste of time. The Ester Police Department just sent out a memo that the video cameras within the bank were disabled moments before the robbery occurred."

"Dammit," Abel shouted. "Thanks for the update, Isabella."

"What about cameras outside of the bank?" I asked.

"As far as I know, cameras outside of the bank were functioning, but inside cameras weren't functioning." Isabella looked at her notepad before leaving the room.

"So, what would you like for us to do?" Jared asked Abel.

"Just head over to 2634 S. Banks and have a talk with Ms. Wilson. We do have her listed as one of the prime suspects capable of pulling this off. You all be careful," he said. "Establish communication once you all arrive."

"On it," Linda said as we all left the room.

I shook hands with Jared and hugged Madeline.

"Don't get fired within your first year," I joked with Jared. "I brought you on board because you've been my boy since first grade."

"I won't leave a sour taste," he chuckled. "You know I got your back though."

"Should we be prepared for anything?" Madeline asked.

"A typical white girl: gotta be prepped for anything," Jared spoke. "You know they're crazy; especially their crimes."

"Right," I spoke.

"Our crimes are getting bad, too." Jared put on his coat. "Back in the day, they were simple. If you didn't have any money, rob someone with some money. But now, these cats are on a killing expedition."

"Back in the day? You only 22, my nigga. What could you know about 'back in the day'?"

"Shit, all I know, is that the white people are the ones with the issues, no offense, Linda."

"Watch it" Linda jokingly fired back as we exited the building.

Jared put his hands up and walked to his car with caution.

"I am walking to my car. That's all I'm doing, Officer," he chuckled as we got closer to our vehicles.

Linda, Madeline, and I all started laughing.

It was clear that this day wasn't going to be stressful working with Jared; as long as his comical spirit didn't give out, everything would be fine. I could manage anything, even my sixth sense.

"Alright, let's first head over to the Flossmoor area for Julie Wilson. We'll see if she's connected to the robbery in some way. Jared, you'll ride with Madeline. You have to collaborate with your new peers as much as possible if you're gonna work here at the station. That leaves you riding with me, Linda."

"Copy," Jared said.

"Let's get a move on" I commanded as everyone paired up for the ride.

2

There was no problem spotting 2634 S. Banks. Like Abel mentioned, the place imitated a mansion's structure and aesthetics, a wide three-story light blue suburban home with an open green lawn. As soon as we arrived in front of the house, I eyed the suspect. With brown bags, she stepped outside of the black suburban, which I noticed had a different license plate. I grabbed my radio.

"Roberts, we are outside of Julie Wilson's residence and have a visual on her. Do you copy?"

Abel bolted with a response, "Copy that, Young. Go on and approach the suspect."

"10-4," I replied as Linda and I got out of my vehicle. "Officers Hubbard and Tucker, stand-by."

"Copy that," Madeline confirmed.

With Linda behind me, I made my way to Julie. She quickly noticed and stared me directly in the eyes. I reacted by showing her my badge.

"Ms. Wilson," I began. "I'm Detective Richard Young and this is my partner, Officer Linda Jackson. We wanted to ask you a few questions."

"Yes, Detective," Julie said, "but I have to get inside. There's dinner in the oven, and I do not want it to burn."

"A little early for dinner, don't you think?" I questioned.

"I'm planning a big feast tonight for my family coming into town," Julie responded in her bright yellow and white polka-dotted dress.

"Isn't there anyone in the house that can watch the food for you?"

Linda asked.

"No, just me, Officer," Julie answered.

"Might you see us inside your home so you can keep an eye on your feast?" I asked.

Julie chuckled nervously, "I would but things are not presentable right now."

Linda took a step towards her. "Ms. Wilson, this will only take a few minutes of your time."

Suddenly, a man in a white shirt and blue jeans walked outside the house.

"Julie," he stated as he made his way to her. He noticed Linda and myself growing impatient. "You didn't tell me you had company."

"And Ms. Wilson told us no one was home," I retorted.

Julie interrupted, "Detective, this is my cousin, Michael Wilson. Michael, this is Detective Young and Officer Jackson. When did you get here?"

"A couple of minutes ago," Michael responded.

"And where did you go this morning," Linda said. "I'm sure it wasn't a store."

"You're right, it wasn't a store," Michael spoke. "I went to the doctor's and then to the bank. I had a few transactions I needed to make," Michael said as he looked me in the eye.

Linda and I look at each other before responding.

"Ms. Wilson, we're going to need for you to come with us down to the station," I spoke as I pulled out my handcuffs.

"You're placing me under arrest? For what?" as she passed the bag to Michael.

"Obstruction of justice," Linda said. "We're conducting an investigation and you're delaying the process. Cuff her and pat her down, Linda."

"You don't have any weapons or anything in your pockets that may harm us, correct?" Linda asked as she placed Julie's arms behind her.

"This can't be happening right now. Are you serious?" Michael said as he speed-walked to Linda.

I stopped him in his tracks.

"Don't worry, Mr. Wilson. If everything checks out, she'll be home in a matter of hours."

Linda put the handcuffs on Julie and walked her to the car.

"Is this legal?" Michael asked while trailing me to the car door.

"It's 100% legal," I said. "If everything checks out, no charges will be pressed and her records shall remain clean. She may be home within a matter of hours."

"You should get back inside and watch the food," Linda stated as she got in the car. I reached inside spoke into the radio.

"Detective Hubbard, please take a snap of subject Michael Wilson. Let's see if he fits our build of suspect number two. If so, we'll be back for him later."

"Already done," Jared spoke.

Michael took walked back to the house in disgust. I got in the car and drove off.

Linda spoke, "As we stated earlier, Ms. Wilson, no charges are being filed at the moment, but if you do not cooperate once we arrive at the station, you will be charged with obstruction of justice."

"I haven't even been Mirandized," Julie retorted, politely.

"Again, you are not charged with any offense for the time being," I sternly objected, making sure this was the last time I repeated myself. "We're just bringing you in for questioning."

I glanced at Julie in the rearview mirror. She tried sitting back in her seat but couldn't because of the handcuffs.

"Well, Detective," she calmly said, "I am willing to cooperate 100% with you."

"Officer Roberts," Linda spoke over the radio. "We are about fifteen minutes away from headquarters."

"10-4," Abel stated over the radio.

I kept looking back at Julie on our way to the station. There was something off about her, but I couldn't put my finger on it.

***

Linda removed the handcuffs from Julie and walked her into the interrogation room; I followed.

"Alright," Julie said while seated. "You all said you had questions for me. Fire away."

Linda began, "Ms. Wilson, I'm sure you heard about the robbery that took place at Ester Communion bank this morning?"

"I've heard something about it," she replied. "I heard they got away with over two million. They lucked their way out with that heist."

"I wouldn't say that," I stated as I pulled out the snapshots that were sent over and put them on the table.

Julie's face turned to stone.

"What, you don't recognize yourself?" Linda said.

"This can't be me," Julie rebutted.

"And why can't it be?" Linda persisted. "Same height, same size, same build. It's like looking in a mirror."

"Is this why you all brought me down here?" Julie asked with her hands placed on her chest. "To interrogate me about a robbery?"

"We're trying to put a few things together," I stated as I walked closer to her, "but you and your truck fit the descriptions seen on the bank's security footage."

"Surely, there is some kind of mistake," Julie said as she got up. "The suspect in the photo may resemble me but come on... that could honestly be anyone in that photo."

"And why couldn't it be you?" Linda was becoming more irritated by the fact that Julie was calm and wasn't buckling.

"I was at the store during the robbery. You all saw the grocery bags. I couldn't be in two places at one time," Julie smirked.

Linda and I both looked at each other.

"Sit back down," I said, "What about Michael?"

Julie sat down with her legs and arms crossed. "What about him?"

"Maybe he has some involvement," Linda said while leaning on the table. "After all, he said he went to the bank to make a few transactions."

"He was getting some money so we can treat our family that's visiting out to dinner," Julie defended.

"I thought you were cooking a big feast for them," I rebutted.

Julie smiled, "Just in case things don't work out, and it looks like things won't because you all keep wasting my time."

"Do you remember a traffic stop in which an officer saw blueprints for a bank?" Linda backtracked to what Abel said in the meeting.

"Okay, I'm a contractor. So, sue me." Julie replied. "Look, I am trying to cooperate, but the more you accuse me of something, the less cooperative I will be."

There was a knock on the one-way glass.

"Excuse me for a second," I said as I exited the room.

"Cut her loose Richard," Abel told me.

"What? Why?" I asked.

"Her alibi checks out. Security cameras have her shopping at the time of the robbery."

"So, we have nothing," I asked him.

"For now, no... Cut her loose," Abel demanded.

I walked back to the room with indifference.

"You're free to go, Ms. Wilson," I stated.

Linda looked at me.

"Captain's orders," I replied.

Julie compiled herself and rose to her feet.

"Thank you for your time," I mentioned as she walked towards the door.

"I hope you all find the suspect that you're looking for," Julie spoke, "I truly do." I saw a smirk on her face one last time as she passed me. A mental image of the future came to me during this.

When Julie left the station, I regrouped with Linda, Jared, and Madeline.

"She robbed that bank," I stated with clarity.

"If the convenience store footage clears her, what are we to do?" Jared asked.

"We have to do a further investigation on this," I said as I headed outside. "She's hiding something."

Linda and Jared followed me.

"And where are you going?" Linda asked.

"I'm going to the convenience store to have a look at the tapes. Something isn't adding up. Remember what I told you happened to me earlier? My sixth sense?"

"Yeah, what about it?" Linda asked.

"It happened again while Julie passed by me. I just know she had something to do with this by the look she gave me as she headed out."

Linda took a beat while Jared nodded at me.

"Okay, let's head over there," Linda spoke, "Stay back for any more clues, Jared."

Linda got in my car before I drove to the convenience store that Julie supposedly went to. I was determined to crack this case.

***

"We're just here to look at the tapes," I told Linda once we arrived.

"Got it," Linda said.

We exited the vehicle and put our guns in our holsters.

"Let me ask you a quick question, Linda, have you ever shot your gun?" I joked.

"Not really, but I'll be quick to use it if I need to," Linda joked back.

"Ah, you may not need to as long as you have me by your side," I assured her.

"I can hold my own," she joked. "Don't tell me that you're trigger happy," Linda replied.

I shrugged my shoulders and proceeded inside with Linda.

We entered the store and saw the associate at the front.

"Sir, I'm Detective Richard Young and this is my partner, Officer Linda Jackson." I pulled out my badge. Linda showed hers as well.

"We're here to take a look at your security tapes," I spoke.

"Give me one moment, Officers. I'll get my manager. I don't have access to the tapes," the associate said as he walked to the back.

"Do you think we'll have any luck?" Linda asked.

"You never know. With any luck, yes," I stated as I leaned on the counter.

The associate returned with a lady.

"Hello, I'm Jalesa Moss, the manager," she wiped her hands on a towel and extended her hand for a handshake, "What can I help you all with?"

"Detective Richard Young," I shook her hand. "We're investigating the bank robbery that took place this morning. A suspect of ours claimed she was in your store during the robbery. We'd like to take a look at your security tapes."

Jalesa displayed a concerned look on her face and spoke.

"Right this way, Detectives," she said.

Jalesa led us to the security room. "These are a lot of screens you have here for a small store," I said as I looked around.

"We need a lot of cameras. People are always trying to come in and shoplift."

"Has anyone ever tried to rob you?" Linda asked.

Jalesa chuckled. "We're a convenience store, Officer. The most we carry in the register at one time is $500 on your average day."

I looked around and pulled out the notepad I carried.

"Can you rewind these tapes to about 9:45 this morning?" I asked.

As the tape rewound, I was looking at the largest monitor in an attempt to find Julie.

"There she is," Linda pointed out. I was surprised to see her on the tape.

"Well, are you satisfied?" Linda asked me.

Jalesa pressed play, and I watched the tape progress forward.

"Do you think it could take us back to about a week ago?" Linda asked.

"This thing could take you back twenty years," Jalesa stated. "Recording 24-7 and storing everything in a private online cloud."

"Let's hope it can give us the answers we need," I spoke.

Jalesa went back to the live screen so that the backup could commence.

I looked at the time currently displayed on the monitor.

"Is it that early?" I asked. "Linda, what time is it?"

"It's 5:45," she spoke.

"Jalesa, this time isn't right," I told her. "This means that your system isn't recording with the correct timestamps."

"I hadn't even noticed, Detective," Jalesa spoke.

"You know it's a crime to lie to law enforcement when they're conducting an investigation." Linda reminded her.

"I'm not obstructing justice," Jalesa pleaded. "Someone must have tampered with the settings."

"These times are about two hours behind," I spoke as I noticed the time showed 3:46 on my phone.

"And you're telling us that you didn't notice this?" Linda questioned again.

"Detective, please," Jalesa begged.

"It's not unnoticeable," I spoke.

"Detective Young, what's a person looking at for obstruction?" Linda asked me.

"Well, it all depends on the seriousness of the investigation that's being conducted. For something like this, five-to-ten." I spoke.

"5-to-10 years in prison; I don't think stripes would do you justice," Linda replied.

Jalesa face displayed a look of concern.

"You seem nervous for someone who doesn't know anything," I stated.

"I don't want to go to jail," Jalesa whispered.

"Tell us something," Linda spoke.

"I don't know anything about any of this," she assured us.

I pulled out my handcuffs and put one of the cuffs on Jalesa's hand.

"Tell us something," Linda reiterated.

"I have just told you all," Jalesa cried.

"Okay," I spoke as I put her hand behind her back and pulled the other arm behind. I began to put her other hand in the cuff, and lock it when she spoke.

"You sure you don't know anything?" Linda asked her.

"Alright!" Jalesa shouted

I stopped locking the handcuffs.

"A few days ago, a woman and man entered the store and said they were here to perform maintenance on the system."

"And?" Linda asked.

"And then, I noticed that the times were off... I've been meaning to change it back, but things have been so busy."

"So, which one is it?" I asked. "At first, you didn't realize the change, and now you know some people came in for maintenance."

"That's all I know," Jalesa said. "I can't do jail time."

I unlocked the handcuffs and removed them from both of her hands.

"We're going to need the names of those people who performed maintenance on the system," Linda spoke.

I passed Jalesa my card, then turned to Linda.

"Officer Jackson, we have to get going. Jalesa, we'll be expecting a call from you with those names," I spoke.

"You should fix the time right now," Linda spoke before following me from the back.

We walked out of the store and to my car.

"I can't believe you just cuffed that woman," Linda laughed.

"I had to get the information out of her, some way. You helped get the information by asking me how long she would get in prison," I chuckled.

"So, let's be clear: if she hadn't told you, would you have arrested her?" Linda asked.

"Hell no I wasn't going to, I was just using the fear of prison to hear what we needed."

"Well, now we know that Julie wasn't actually here during the robbery," Linda said.

I started the engine.

"Which means that she could have easily robbed that bank," I spoke as I drove away.

"Where to next?" Linda asked me.

"We're stopping by the bank for a moment. Surely, we can find some evidence, and talk to some people about it."

Linda picked up the transmitter to the radio.

"This is Officer Jackson, shield number 2816, currently with Detective Young, shield number 4352. We are en route to Ester Communion Bank. Requesting additional units."

"10-4, additional units in route to the Ester Communion Bank," the dispatcher replied.

I turned the car around and drove towards the bank.

"What's the likelihood that we could find anything that puts Julie at the scene of the crime?" Linda asked as I sped towards the bank.

"I have a pretty good feeling about this," I spoke to Linda.

We arrived at the bank and police vehicles were parked outside of the bank; not only Chicago police department vehicles, but as well as Ester police vehicles.

"Alright, Linda, let's only focus on the task at hand. Do not try to compete with the Ester PD. You know that they're going to have their heads held high because it is their town and they're going to feel like it's their case."

"Even though we've been assigned to the case as well..."

"It's a pride thing," I told her.

We walked into the bank and saw yellow tape all around.

Linda and I pulled out our badges.

We walked over to some of the officers.

"What have we got here?" I asked.

"We're dusting this section for fingerprints," the officer stated. "They caused a lot of damage to the bank."

"Any injuries or fatalities?" Linda asked.

"No injuries or fatalities. We can see that wasn't their motive. They fired a few blank shots in the air, which have left us with the shell casings."

I looked at the shattered windows and glass on the carpet, as well as the pillar that was knocked down on the far end of the bank.

"Damn, did they cause all of this damage?" I asked the officer.

"The driver drove the getaway car through the north end of the bank, paused for a second for the robber to get in the vehicle, and exited through the south end."

"Okay, well surely surveillance must have captured something," I spoke.

"I will check with the manager of the bank about getting the footage from the cameras outside of the bank. We are also checking with local businesses to get any footage they may have captured of the getaway."

Linda and I walked away from the officers towards the front desk.

"Mam, I'm Detective Young from the Chicago PD; this is my partner, Officer Jackson."

"How are you officers doing today? I'm Jennifer Lawrence, the manager," she spoke.

"Everything is alright on our end. I wish we could say the same about you all. How are you holding up?" I asked Jennifer.

The woman grabbed a folder and walked from behind the counter.

"I don't get it; the whole bank is destroyed in a matter of seconds. Not even a full three minutes passed, and the woman was in and out."

"So, you can confirm that it was a woman who robbed you?" Linda asked.

"A woman robbed the bank and a man drove the getaway vehicle, I think. Trust me, no matter how you try to cover up, you can tell a woman's shape over a man's." Jennifer stopped at the desk and turned around. "So, unless it was a gay guy who has a fabulous shape and can sound like a woman, I can guarantee you that it was a woman."

Linda and I looked at each other as the woman continued to walk.

"You see this glass." Jennifer pointed at the glass on the floor. "Bullet-resistant glass for all windows. Never once did I expect someone to drive through it," Jennifer threw the folder with papers on the floor and screamed out of disgust. "Fuck!"

"Jennifer, calm down," Linda said. "We guarantee that you have the best law enforcement team working on this case to try to reclaim everything that was yours."

"Do you have an exact amount of how much was taken in today's robbery?" I asked her.

"All of that is calculated upstairs with the financial department. Security system is also located upstairs."

"So, tell me, did the woman just walk in the bank with a rifle?" Linda asked.

"Damnedest thing," she began, "no one saw her enter the bank at all."

"That's because she didn't enter through the front," a security guard stated as he came down the stairs.

"How's it going up there, Henry?" she asked.

"It's a real mess. We just went into the maintenance room, you know, where the electrical equipment all ties together. Glass is everywhere. The motion camera caught her as she came in."

Henry passed each of us a set of images. Linda and I looked at the images in our hands.

"Camera took a shot of a helicopter hovering above, and it shows her jumping from a helicopter and in through the glass ceiling of that room."

"Does this camera capture video?" I asked Henry.

"At the moment, this camera only captures images but takes each image back-to-back once it detects motion. So, kind of like video, but not exactly."

"Jennifer, can you take us upstairs and to this room; Henry, we need for you to pull the exact amount of money that was taken today," I spoke.

"Sure, Detectives, follow me," she spoke as she walked upstairs.

Linda and I followed her but made sure not to touch anything.

She opened the door to the maintenance room. Shattered glass covered the floor and computer towers.

"And no one heard all of this glass break?" Linda asked.

"Things have been so busy around here. There's a chance that no one was around when she fell through."

I looked up to the ceiling that was now broken.

"Jennifer, can you take us to the roof? I want to take a look at the camera that captured her coming in." I spoke.

"No problem," she spoke as she walked out of the door and to the far end of the bank.

She pulled out her key-card and swiped it before opening another door.

"This door locks from the inside and out," she spoke as she walked up the stairs that led to the roof.

"Watch your step," Linda spoke as we walked on the roof.

"Where's the camera?" I asked Jennifer.

"You're standing in front of it." She chuckled. "One of the beauties of this camera, it captures things in all directions: horizontal, vertical, and diagonal."

I kneeled and looked at the camera, which didn't even look like a camera. It resembled a light bulb, that wasn't lit.

"Yea, the suspect wouldn't have known she was being monitored from the roof," I spoke. "Let's get forensics up here to take pictures and dust for footprints, etc."

Linda spoke into the transmitter and called for forensics to come up and swab for evidence.

"Well, I'll admit that the criminal went all out and thought about this. By the pictures that Henry has given us, it didn't capture any descriptive information about the helicopter, except for the VIN number."

"We have our work cut out for us," Linda spoke.

"And I'm dedicated to working around the clock until we catch these people," I retorted.

"As I've told you before; you have the best team in the city working hard to solve this case," Linda reminded Jennifer.

We walked back down the stairs and into the bank. Henry approached us.

"Detectives, we've gotten those numbers for you." He spoke.

"Okay, what's the total amount?" Linda asked as she pulled her notepad out of her pocket.

"They took north of 2 million. Exactly $2,923,635."

"That's a lot of money," I spoke.

"That's a lot of customer's accounts," Jennifer spoke.

A radio transmission came through that called for Linda and me.

"Alright Ms. Lawrence, you gave us enough information, but we ask that you send over all of the snapshots to our station so that we can further look into this robbery," Linda said as she extended a hand to Jennifer.

I extended my hand to Henry.

"I will pull the screenshots and send them over to the station," Jennifer replied as I pulled out my card.

"We'll be in touch," I spoke as Linda and I walked away.

We both got in my car and I drove towards the police station.

"So, if Julie used a helicopter, surely she has to have a connection with a pilot or someone with experience in flying." I merged onto the expressway.

"So, we should run a cross on all of her affiliations; her cousin, and any friends or family who can fly or has access to a helicopter," Linda unloaded her gun and put the clip in her pocket.

"Exactly," I spoke.

"It's almost 8," Linda spoke as she yawned.

"Thinking about turning in?" I asked her.

"It's been a long day," she spoke.

"Yea, but we haven't really poked any holes in the case." I pulled into the police station parking lot.

"We can get a fresh start on Monday," Linda spoke. "I still have to get home and get things ready."

I let out a sigh.

"Well, I'm gonna just stay here and work a bit more," I got out of the car.

Linda loaded her gun as we walked into the station.

"Any news?" Abel asked as we walked past him.

"Quite a bit. However, we still can't point fingers at Julie and her cousin." I started. "We know the exact total that was taken, and we know how the suspect entered the bank."

"They used a helicopter, Abel," Linda spoke.

"A helicopter?" he spoke.

"Cameras on the roof got a glimpse of the chopper and the woman rappelling down through the glass roof of the maintenance room," I spoke. "Jennifer should be sending over the snapshots the camera captured, as well as any other info we may need to solve this."

"Well, while we're waiting on those, let's keep an eye on Ms. Wilson. We cannot let her leave the city or get out until we have completely ruled her out as a suspect," Abel spoke. He looked at the clock. "It's about that time. Any big plans for the night?" he changed the topic.

"Just go home and get ready for Monday," Linda spoke. "Since we have Sundays off, I just need to go cook and clean my house before I sleep tonight."

"Not for tonight," I declared. "I'm gonna do a little more for this case."

"Determined, huh? I like that," Abel spoke. He walked into his office and grabbed his coat before turning off the light and closing the door.

Linda and I stood by his door.

"Don't forget to do an inventory check of your weapons and badges before you leave, and I will see you all on Monday," Abel stated as he shook my hand. He shook Linda's hand and left the building.

"You heading out?" I asked Linda.

"Yea, I'm getting on out of here," she spoke as she grabbed her coat.

"Alright, Linda," I shook her hand. "I'm gonna head back here and get some more work done on this case. Just keep an eye on Julie. Can't let her walk until it's done," I spoke.

"Will do," she walked to the front to do a check of her weapons and ammo.

I walked to my office and closed the door.

***

Two hours later, there was a knock on my door. I looked back and waved for the officer to enter.

"Damn, you're still here, Rick?" Jared asked.

"Yeah, I'm trying to find out as much as I can about this case." I ruffled through the papers on my desk.

Jared looked at them and picked up some of the screenshots.

"Did this woman really use a helicopter in the robbery?" Jared chuckled.

"Whoever did this definitely knew the inner workings of the bank. They knew exactly how to enter without anyone noticing, they knew exactly where they would end up by rappelling through the ceiling, and everything was plotted perfectly." I shook my head.

"Did you all find out exactly how much was taken?"'

"Yea," I began to shuffle through the papers. "$2,923,635 was taken from the bank. Abel doesn't want this woman to leave town," I spoke.

"Well then, we don't let her," Jared spoke.

"My dog," I spoke as I put the papers into a folder and put the folder into my book-bag.

Jared left my office and I closed the door as I walked out.

We checked our weapons at the front and walked to our vehicles.

"So, what's the plan?" Jared asked over the phone.

"Thinking of a stake-out?" I asked.

"You mean you wanna camp out in front of her house all night?" Jared asked.

"You got something else planned?" I asked him.

"Nah, I'm down," he spoke.

"Let's do it then," I spoke as I left the parking lot and drove over to Julie's house; Jared followed.

"So, what's the plan, Rick?" Jared asked over the radio as we parked the car.

"Nothing we can do. Kill your engine and let's just wait," I spoke. "Hopefully we can have enough to convict this girl of the crime."

I heard Jared yawn over the radio.

"Let's do it."

I turned my radio down and picked up my coffee. I sipped and stared at Julie's door.

3

The next day arrived with Jared and me still outside of Julie's home.

"Damn, I stink," Jared said.

"That's what camping in a car for twenty-one hours does to you," I joked. "Just suck it up."

"So, give it to me straight," Jared spoke. "What makes you think this chick is responsible for the bank robbery?"

"Alright, man. Since we're brothers, I'll let you in on this. At any moment, I have 'episodes' where I can see into the future. I don't know if I was born with this condition, but it kicked in yesterday morning. And wanna know what was my first vision? Two criminals leaving the Ester Communion Bank in a black suburban."

"Damn," Jared spoke. "Well, so much for throwing you a surprise party for your birthday. But what makes you think that Ms. Wilson is responsible for the robbery?"

"Remember when Linda and I were interviewing her?" I said.

"Well, another image came to me, and it confirmed that Julie was involved with this robbery."

"So, I can see you're set on doing whatever it takes to catch this woman," Jared said.

"By any means necessary," I replied. "Including camping out in a car with your bum ass."

Jared laughed. Soon, he pointed to the house. Julie came out of the door.

"There's your girl," Jared said.

"Yep, there she goes," I spoke as I sat up.

Julie looked both ways before walking down the steps.

"The fuck is she looking for?" I whispered.

"Should we follow her?" Jared asked.

"Not yet," I replied as she walked by the flowers in the front yard.

She continued to look around at the vehicles on her street.

"We're on the other side of the street," I spoke. "She's not going to make us." I looked at Julie.

"Look at her: same height and build as the bank robber and she has the means to do it by having that blueprint."

"You wanna just bust her?" Jared asked.

"I don't want to spook her. Besides, I'd rather take her head-on with backup."

"Understood," Jared uttered as he saw Michael coming out of the house. "You remember him?"

"Michael Wilson, her cousin. He doesn't have a rap sheet with the law either."

"What about him? Does he fit the profile of the second accomplice?"

"I can't really tell. There are no images of the accomplice outside of the vehicle."

"Let's run a cross on Julie and see if she has access to a helicopter or anyone who knows how to fly," Jared pulled out the laptop.

He typed 'Wilson, Julie' into the search field, but no results came back.

I took a moment to myself.

Who the hell are we dealing with?

***

It was the second morning camped outside Julie's house. I opened my eyes and saw the black suburban was still in front. Julie walked outside to check her mailbox.

I tapped Jared; he woke up slowly.

"J, wake up."

"Damn, we're still in this car?"

"You already know. Let's request a unit come by and we head home to freshen up. Forty-five hours in a car is not the way to go," I chuckled.

Jared picked up the microphone.

"This is Detective Hubbard. Requesting a unit come and keep an eye on one, Julie Wilson."

"10-4. We have a unit on the way."

"Requesting under-cover, unmarked car," Jared added.

"10-4." The dispatcher spoke.

Jared got out of my car and spoke through the passenger window.

"So, what's the plan?" he asked.

"Let's head to our homes and take a shower and get cleaned up. Then, we head back out here to take Julie in for questioning." I told him.

"I gotcha," he spoke as he tapped the door and walked to his car.

He got inside and started the engine. I started mine and drove off.

I arrived home moments later and walked inside. I took a shower and put on some fresh clothes.

One of the best parts of this job. You could wear whatever, as long as it was appropriate and comfortable.

I got in the car and called Jared.

"Yo, I'm heading back to her home. Where are you?" I asked.

"Getting back in my car now," Jared spoke. "I'll see you there."

I picked up the microphone and send a transmission to Abel.

"Young to Roberts. I repeat, Young to Roberts."

"Roberts, here," he replied.

"Currently in route to Julie Wilson's residence. Detective Hubbard and I are going to bring her in for a second set of questioning about the robbery."

"10-4, you all be careful," he spoke.

"Let's do it," Jared spoke over the radio.

***

"Ms. Wilson?" I called as I knocked on her door.

Julie opened the door slowly.

"What do you all want now?" Julie sighed out.

"We need for you to come down to the station with us," Jared said.

Julie was in shock. "Didn't I tell you all before that I was at the store at the time of the robbery?"

"Your alibi doesn't check out," I said.

Julie had a serious look on her face.

"Those security cameras were off by 2 hours," I added. "So, we're going to need for you to come with us."

Julie looked behind her. "Michael, I have to go down to the police station with these detectives. I'll be back." Julie closed the door.

"The handcuffs will not be necessary," Julie mentioned.

This time, I didn't force the necessity of the handcuffs.

"So, where's the car?" she asked.

"Right this way," I said as I got behind her.

She got in the back seat of my vehicle and I closed the door. I got in the driver's seat and drove off.

Jared got in his car and followed.

The drive was silent, but I made sure to keep my eye on Julie through the rearview mirror, especially since she wasn't in handcuffs.

***

"Where's the money, Julie?" Jared asked as he slammed his hands on the table.

"I don't know what the hell you're talking about," Julie said in a calm tone.

Jared threw some of the screenshots on the table.

"It's like looking in a mirror," Jared whispered.

I watched Jared as he interrogated Julie; I didn't say a word. I made sure I paid attention to the way Julie was reacting.

"Yeah, a very, very dim, and dirty mirror," Julie retorted.

"This has your name written all over it," Jared shouted.

"Calm down, Jared," I said, breaking my silence.

"Detective, wasn't there a woman assisting you, previously?" Julie asked.

"Save it, Julie," I said. I pointed to one of the images. "This is you."

Julie looked at the image. "Crashing down through glass?" she asked.

"Entering the bank," I replied.

"I've already told you, I wasn't there," Julie awkwardly chuckled.

I began, "you know what's funny? You say you were at a store when we have proof that you weren't in that store. The store manager told us all about you coming into the store days before and changed the time on the security tapes."

"I never did such a thing" Julie spoke.

"Bullshit," Jared retorted.

"I'm not lying to you," Julie chuckled.

"Why are you laughing?" I asked her. "You think armed robbery is a joke? What about 10-15 in jail?"

"Fuck that," Jared spoke. "I'm going for the max since she thinks this shit is funny."

"Okay, first thing. You all never said I was under arrest, so, technically, I am free to leave at any given moment. Second, you said you had a few questions for me; not to interrogate me and charge me with a crime that you honestly have no proof that I've committed. The way I see it, I'm going to walk out of that door, nice and easy, because I haven't done a thing wrong." Julie began to rise from the chair.

A knock came from the glass and I walked out of the room.

"Don't move," Jared demanded.

"Sorry, I'm late," Linda spoke as she approached us.

"That's alright," Abel said. He directed his attention to me. "These results came back", he started. "Forensics determined the shoe size that broke in the bank, the kind of gun that was used based off of the shell casings and recovered this strand of hair from the crime scene."

"The bombshell to this case," I spoke.

"Get her shoe size, I'll work on getting a warrant for her home, and get a swab of her DNA. If her shoe size fits, arrest her and put her in a holding cell. If her DNA is a match, we'll slap these charges on her."

A feeling of slight relief overcame me.

I walked back into the room and pulled out my handcuffs.

"Am I supposed to be intimidated?" Julie asked with a smirk.

"What's going on?" Jared asked.

"Forensics confirm a direct match between the suspect and evidence collected from the crime scene."

A slight smile came across Jared's face; Julie displayed a puzzled expression.

"Jared, please get her shoe size."

"I'm a 7 in women's," Julie sharply responded.

I approached her slowly. "Julie Wilson, you are under arrest for the robbery of the Ester Communion Bank."

"Are you serious right now?" Julie shouted.

I continued while walking behind her and putting the handcuffs on.

"You have the right to remain silent. Anything you say can and will be used against you in the court of law. You have the right to an attorney. If you cannot afford an attorney, one will be appointed to you."

"The fuck, man?" Julie shouted. "Can I get my phone call?"

I ignored her question.

"We will need a swab of DNA as well," I told Jared.

I walked Julie out of the room and into a holding cell. While closing the cell, I noticed that her grin surfaced back on her face.

I stared at her, "I wonder if you'll keep that smirk after the charges are filed."

Julie said nothing. She just stared at me with her curved mouth.

I headed for Abel's office to discuss the evidence.

"We got her," I announced.

"This just came in for you," Abel said as he handed me a piece of paper.

"What's this?" I asked.

"That," he sipped his coffee, "has two names on it that was faxed over by Jalesa Moss."

"Sabrina Brown and Mikael Brown," I read. "These are the names of the people that came in to 'fix' the security system, a few days ago."

"Those security systems were off by a few hours, correct?" Abel asked.

"Yes," I replied, "which is exactly why we have Julie Wilson now in a cell."

"Well, we're getting DNA from her to see if it places her at the scene," Abel replied.

"That reminds me," I said walking towards the door, "we need to cross-reference all of Julie Wilson's family and associates and see who has access to a helicopter."

"Yes, that's crucial to know. See if you can find any leads," he said.

I left the office and passed by the holding cell.

"Detective," Julie called, "could you come here a second?"

I looked at her and walked over.

"How long have you been working here?" she asked.

"Cut the crap, Julie," I said with a stern look.

"I just wanted to know" Julie replied, "um, when can I get my phone call?"

"We'll give you all of that, but it doesn't quite look like you're going anywhere," I told her.

"It wasn't me," Julie said smiling and chuckling.

"You can't fool me, Julie," I said.

With her cold blue yes, Julie stared at me. "In time," she began, "you'll learn the truth. I don't think the CPD would look good with a rap on them for wrongful arrest, considering all of the incidents that currently give them, and the city, a bad taste. So many crimes are being committed right now, and you're arresting me for robbing a bank—that you can't prove I had any involvement in."

I turned away from Julie and I walked into Jared's office. I could hear Julie laughs during my exit.

"Have you pulled those records for me?" I asked a computer-attached Jared.

"Just got this cross-check back. Nothing on her credit report that would indicate spending on an aerial unit and there are no signs that she has any affiliations with someone who can fly."

"Do you know what's going on with the DNA information?"

"They've swabbed her, and should have the results back in a few hours," Jared spoke.

"So, I'm assuming that we should wait for the results to take her down to arraignment," I said.

"Unless you want to add a bad rep to our department," Jared joked.

"Well, Jared, we don't need any more bad publicity," I said as I sat down.

"We may be here for a while," Jared said, typing away.

Suddenly, Linda walked in.

"Is it true?" Linda asked.

"You mean, is *it* true?" Jared said before I could answer.

"Yeah," Linda replied

"You really wanna know?" Jared said, looking up.

"That's why I'm asking, Jared," Linda replied.

"Okay, yes," Jared spoke. "*It's* true."

"How was it?" Linda asked.

"I don't know; just like any other, I guess."

Linda displayed a confused expression on her face.

"Nah, I'm just messing with you," Jared chuckled. "I don't even know what you're talking about."

I snickered but maintained my composure.

"It's something wrong with you," I told Jared.

Linda shook her head. "I'm asking if you all really camped out at Julie's house all day, yesterday."

"Yeah, and it was not fun," I said. "Have you ever spent two full days with someone, in a small space?"

"Don't lie, you know you had fun," Jared joked.

"Yea, right. Being trapped with you for 40 plus hours is never any fun, I laughed.

"What did you all find out?" Linda asked inquisitively.

"Didn't find out anything," I mentioned. "We were just keeping an eye to make sure she didn't try to flee and didn't do anything suspicious."

"Yeah, we did learn one thing," Jared protested. "We learned how boring of a woman Julie is, or at least pretends to be."

"Probably planning her next hit," Linda declared.

"We're waiting on the DNA results for confirmation so that we can take her down to arraignment."

"Let's hope it comes back soon," Linda spoke.

"Hey, can't you have like, a vision or something, and predict this shit?" Jared asked.

"It doesn't quite work like that. It just happens when it wants. Primarily when I don't want it to."

"Try to learn to get it under control," Linda said. "It could come in handy."

***

An hour later, there was a tap on my office window.

"Come in," I said looking at the door.

The door cracked open; it was Abel poking his head in.

"Results are in," he said.

I got up and walked with Abel over to the interview room. Jared and Olivia, our technician, occupied the area.

"So, what do we have?" I asked.

"I had to bring these results up here, personally," Olivia said as she pulled a white paper out of the manila envelope. "This is the DNA that was collected from the crime scene, and this," she removed another piece of paper, "is Julie's DNA."

"They're identical," I said with confidence.

"Correct, they are identical, but they aren't a match." Olivia put the two strips of paper over one another. "Notice how they don't line up with each other."

"So, what do you think this means?" Jared asked.

"From looking at this," Olivia said holding the papers closer to the ceiling light, "I'd say that this hair found does not belong to Ms. Wilson. While it doesn't mean that she wasn't at the bank, it does mean that she is closely related to whomever the hair belongs to; either a father, a brother or even a cousin. But one thing's certain. This hair belongs to a male."

"You hear that, Linda?" I asked.

"Thanks, Olivia," Abel said. He turned to me, "Gotta cut her loose again, Richard."

"Abel, we still have the warrant to search her place for the weapon and shoes used," I said, wanting to close this case for good.

"Yea, and that's all we have," Abel said walking away. "The D.A. isn't going to hold her with iffy evidence."

"Fuck," I whispered under my breath as I walked towards the holding cell.

Julie was laying on the bench asleep.

"Julie Wilson," I called and woke her up.

She rubbed her eyes and sat up. She looked around and noticed she was still in the cell.

"Detective," she replied with a smile. "How are you?"

"You're free to go," I said, reluctantly.

Julie rose to her feet.

"Did *your* story not check out?" Julie asked.

I opened the cell and let her walk past me.

"I think you need to get laid, or something," Julie said. "A little too much tension in your body."

"You keep up those comments and I'll throw you back in this cell," I told her as she walked towards the front.

She got her belongings and walked out of the police station.

"So, now what?" Jared asked.

"I don't even know where to start," I said holding my head.

Jared patted me on the shoulder.

"Don't stress over it," he retorted.

I stood there and thought about what Olivia just told us. I walked over to Abel's office.

"Roberts, I'm requesting that we go and pick up Michael Wilson," I said.

"Negative," he quickly said. "I'm waiting to get this search warrant to go into her home, but I don't want you or any other officer to go near that woman," he continued. "The last thing we need is for her to be claiming the Chicago Police Department harassed her."

I gestured my hands in the direction of the DNA room.

"But you heard what Olivia said: the hair belongs to an immediate relative of Julie Wilson."

"I don't care," Abel said with a blank stare, "We don't move until this warrant comes back."

I put my hands on my head.

With a head-start, Julie's gonna alert her cousin about the heat coming down on them.

I walked into Jared's office.

"I need you to be ready. As soon as Roberts gets this warrant, we need to be set to go in for this bust."

"What are you anticipating?" Jared asked as he lowered the music playing from his computer.

"Julie got a head-start out of here," I told him.

"Okay..." Jared said, unsure of what I meant.

"And Olivia said the hair belonged to an immediate male relative; such as a cousin."

"So, you think she's alerting Michael and they're about to get the fuck out of dodge?"

"That's exactly what I'm thinking. Julie's been playing this game with us and making us run around trying to gather this evidence." I thought for a moment. "Jared, run a search on Michael Wilson and find out if he knows how to fly. It could be an airplane, a helicopter, a private jet, I don't care. I just need to know if he knows how to fly. If I find out that he does, we can put him inside as the pilot of the helicopter."

Jared sat up in his seat.

"Let's close this case," he stated as he shook my hand.

I walked out of his office and returned to my desk.

"You think you're slick," I stated as I looked at the picture of the suspect as she entered the bank. "Got you, now."

***

"We got the warrant," Abel announced an hour later.

I was the first to respond to the memo; I picked up my keys from my table.

"Everyone rides with their assigned parties," Isabella stated aloud.

"The moment you've been waiting for?" Jared asked as he power-walked out of the police station next to me.

"You already know," I stated.

Linda waited beside my vehicle and I shook hands with Jared, as we parted ways.

I unlocked the car door and Linda got inside.

"Let's keep this simple," I stated over the radio.

"You ready?" Linda asked me.

I revved my engine in reply.

"Guess so," she stated as she put on her seatbelt.

I followed the other police vehicles as they left the lot with their sirens on.

Transmissions began to sound off over the radio.

"Keep an ear for anything about Julie," I instructed Linda as all of the officers got closer to reaching Julie's home.

"There's a lot of information," Linda spoke as she listened closely to the radio.

A few seconds later, a transmission came through.

"All units, be advised. Reports of a disturbance at Julie Wilson's residence. Proceed with caution."

"That's the memo," Linda spoke.

"Alright, we go in clean. Let's leave all units on the ground. Officer Jackson and I will enter the residence with the warrant. Once we get in, we will alert the rest of the officers to enter." I spoke over the radio.

"10-4," Jared spoke over the radio as we all turned down Julie's street.

All of the officers emerged from the vehicles and unloaded.

Linda and I walked over to Abel.

"You all be safe," he spoke as two officers tightened the bullet-proof vests on Linda and me.

He handed me the warrant.

"Once you all get into the home, make sure you send a transmission for the rest to enter."

"Will do," I spoke as Linda pulled out her weapon.

We both walked up to the door.

"Julie Wilson," I began said while pounding on the door, "this is Detective Richard Young of the Chicago Police Department. We have a search warrant." By the third knock, the door opened by itself. I immediately pulled out my gun. I looked at Linda and nodded. We entered the home with caution.

"Julie Wilson," I shouted holding my gun up in a house cloaked in darkness.

There was no response.

I whispered to Linda while pointing to the left with my head. "Scope out that area and stay alert. She might be playing another cat and mouse game with us."

Linda nodded and crouched her way towards the desired space. Meanwhile, I noticed a door upstairs.

"I'm taking a look upstairs," I voiced as loud as I thought Linda could hear me while moving undetected. "Remember, stay alert."

I slowly made my way to the stairs, using my gun to look in every direction possible. From the stairs' creaking with each step, I clinched the gun tighter. Sweat trickled down the back of my neck from every violent scenario playing through my mind. I finally reached the bedroom but in a crowd of silence. Gripping the Smith and Wesson with one hand, I twisted the doorknob with the other. As soon as I heard a click from the knob, I flew down the stairs and landed on my back next to the house's entrance. I only heard ringing in my ears, but I still apprehended a frightened Linda screaming on her radio. I gazed upstairs and noticed the bedroom engorged with flames.

Linda ran to me and placed her gun back in the holster. "Explosion," Linda screeched, "10-00. I repeat, 10-00, officer down. Requesting backup."

Linda returned the microphone to her shoulder and spoke to me.

"Shit, your leg. We have to get you out of here."

Linda lifted my arm and placed it over her shoulder. Suddenly, another vision came to me.

I was lying in a hospital bed covered with balloons and flowers. Linda sat next to me and Jared and Madeline were across the room. Perfect.

I closed my eyes. I limped out of death in style.

4

"In breaking news, an explosion occurred during an authorized home search on the 4600 block of Banks. The home belonged to Julie and Michael Wilson. The homeowners were not present; however, their whereabouts are unknown. Police suspect that the Wilsons played a role in the Ester Bank robbery that occurred earlier this week. Zero casualties are reported from the explosion, but there is a confirmed injury. Detective Richard Young of the Chicago Police Department is undergoing treatment for severe burns and leg pain. We'll keep you updated on this and more as the story unfolds."

Linda turned and noticed that my eyes were open. "He's awake!"

Jared and Madeline turned to me and sprinted to the bed.

"How you feeling, bro?" Jared asked.

"I can't feel my left leg," I whispered. "Shit, what happened?"

"You passed out after the explosion," Linda said. "They gotta perform surgery on your leg. You got a couple of fractures."

"Did they find Julie and Michael?" I asked.

"Negative," said Madeline. "We haven't heard from them nor have we seen them since we released Julie."

"Dammit!" I shouted, shaking my head while examining the broken leg. "This is exactly what I feared would happen if we let her walk.

"Is the morphine working?" Madeline asked as she looked at the machine.

"Something's working, 'cause I honestly can't feel shit," I responded as I looked at the IV tubes in my arm.

The doctor entered the room with a few nurses behind him. I looked at his nameplate and read 'S. Glisen'.

"Somebody's awake," Dr. Glisen said looking at me with a smile. He gazed at the machines and took my vitals. "Your leg has a few fractures, so, I'm ordering surgery. Following surgery, we'll have to put you in a cast."

"What time is the surgery?" I asked.

"Let me check," the doctor flipped some pages on the clipboard. "We have you at 3 pm; it's 10 am now. Just sit back and relax until then. Anything I can get you?"

I looked down, "A new leg."

Doctor Glisen smiled as he started to leave the room, "well, call if you need anything, Detective."

The cardiac monitor talked for a moment before Linda chimed in. "Where could Julie and her brother be hiding?"

"Well, Linda," I began while adjusting. "You know you have to take over the case while I'm in here."

"Think you can handle it on your own?" Jared teased.

"I'm a big girl, I'll be fine," Linda joked. She looked at me, "I want to make sure you're okay before moving forward."

I looked at the clock on the wall. "I have about five hours until surgery; I should be fine. Though, Abel will want to reexamine the house for any leads."

Just as I finished my remark, my phone rang.

"Roberts," I answered.

"Young, so glad you're not dead," Abel said with a laugh.

"Alive and well," I replied with a chuckle. "Surgery is in a few hours."

"That's good," said Abel. "So, you should be back on your feet in no time."

"Linda, Jared, and Madeline are all here," I said while looking at the television for news updates on the explosion. "Any word on Julie?"

"Haven't had any leads or tips on them. I need someone to go back to the house and look around for evidence."

I knew it. You're a predictable man, Roberts.

"I gotta theory about those bastards fleeing," I spoke.

"What ya got?" Abel asked.

I began, "Julie heard so much talk about a search warrant at the station, that she went back home and warned Michael. Preparing for the authorized search, the two planted an explosive that would destroy anything possibly convicting them of the bank robbery. Knowing the house would be destroyed, the two had no other choice but to leave."

"Hmm," Abel said. "That's a good theory, Young, but we still need concrete evidence."

"Want me to send Linda that way?" I asked.

"Yes. She can meet up with the forensic team at the house," said Abel. "Take it easy."

"Will do", I replied. I hung up.

I looked at Linda. "Roberts wants you to head over there with the forensics team to check it out."

"Well, let me get right on that," Linda said putting on her police vest. "I'll call you in a bit."

She nodded to Jared and Madeline before exiting the hospital.

5

-Linda

"Officer Jackson," shouted a forensics team member as I walked onto the crime scene.

"What you got for me, Connor?" I asked.

Officer Connor scanned the team behind him while talking.

"We determined the form of explosive used and planted."

"So, you're saying this was intentional," I declared.

"Well," Connor began, turning back in my direction, "forensics confirmed that the explosive was set to arm once the motion sensor detected movement and the door opening triggered the explosion."

"That's a crime in itself," I said.

Connor signed, "I just hope we catch these people before they strike again."

"Well, did you all dust for prints?" I asked, raising an eyebrow.

"Ultimately, there's nothing to dust," Connor said. "Most of it was destroyed in the explosion. Forensics are still dusting a few things, such as the explosive, the doors, etc."

"Let me know what you come up with," I replied before walking off. Aiming for what was left of the house, flashbacks from last night clouded my sight. Reaching the threshold, I envisioned dragging Richard out of the flames. Though I was a bit injured, I knew I was in better shape compared to my partner.

"I hope you make a speedy recovery Richard. I really do," I spoke aloud.

Many items and appliances were scattered on the kitchen floor after the explosion, yet a perfectly folded note, as if placed, caught my eyes. I kneeled over the note but was hesitant to pick it up. Looking up, I saw Officer Brown viewing the kitchen counter.

"Officer Brown," I called.

He took a break from examining and turned to me. "Yes, Officer Jackson."

"You all place this here?" I asked.

"Not that I know of," Officer Brown replied. "I can get forensics over here for fingerprints."

"Send them over," I said, reaching in my pocket for latex gloves. Finally, I opened the note and read it aloud. "4:30 at I-290 West South Canal St 5630 D5."

Intrigued at the note and worried about Richard, I called Jared back at the hospital.

Jared answered. "Hey, Linda. What's the status?"

"Forensics team deemed the bombing intentional," I replied.

"Hell, we could've declared that with Richard in bed," Jared said

"I also found a note on the counter," I continued.

"Oooooo, is it a love note?" Jared asked.

"No," I chuckled. I held the note to my face. "It says '4:30, I-290 West 5630 South Canal Street 5630'. Any idea what it means?"

Jared took a minute before replying. "I'm no expert, but I think it's just saying where their next spot will be. Don't go for the attack. Radio Roberts and let him know the status."

I looked away from the note. "Once I let Roberts know what's going on, I'll check-in and see what we're going to do."

"Let's do it," Jared said.

"Jared," I shouted on the phone. "How's Richard?"

"He's doing fine, getting plenty of rest," Jared assured.

I smiled. "Alright, I'll see you soon Jared."

I hung up and bolted out of the house. At my car, I established contact with Abel, disclosing the note, and the lead Jared and I thought of.

"Alright, Jackson, report back to the station," Abel said. "Tonight, we're going to go in for a raid."

"Copy that," I said. "I'm going to check in with Young, and head to the station."

"Over and out," Abel said.

I got in my car as soon as Abel hung up the phone. Before taking off, I called Jared.

"Yo," Jared said.

"Roberts went with the lead. We're raiding the location." I said while driving off.

"Hell yeah," Jared said. "Richard's about to go into surgery. Wanna talk to him before he goes in?"

"Give him the phone," I said.

"Hey, Linda," Richard said.

"Rick!" I joyfully yelled. "Are you ready to get back on your feet?"

"Hell yeah," Richard chuckled. "They should be coming to get me in a few moments; the nurse just left out."

"I know it'll go well," I said. We're going to raid the address posted on a note I found at the house tonight."

"Keep me posted on what happens," Richard said.

The nurse entered the room.

"I'll have to call you back, Linda. They're about to take me down for surgery."

"Good luck," I said before hanging up.

* * *

I arrived at the police station with full energy. I got out of the car and rushed into the station.

Abel greeted me as I walked through the door.

"Officer Jackson," he called as I checked my weapon with the front security.

I walked over to him while the other officers followed me, presumably for instructions for the raid.

"Do you have the address?" Abel asked me.

"Here's what was on the note," I took out the note concealed in a clear bag and showed him.

"Alright, people," Abel began, "head over to S. Canal Street to lock away these scumbags. Move!"

SWAT team members rushed out of the building and to their truck; officers, including myself, did the same. Abel led us in the drive.

I picked up my radio and gave out orders. "Be on high alert. Approach the area with caution."

"10-4," the dispatcher replied. "Officers in route to the Wilson residence, silent sirens."

As we arrived at the address, my heart started to beat fast and my palms got sweaty.

Are we gonna finally apprehend Julie and Michael, or are we rushing into another death trap?

As we drove down the block, I noticed there weren't any vehicles on the street.

"Street cleaning?" I asked over the radio as I parked my car.

"No signs posted or anything; just take extreme caution when entering the building," an officer replied.

I got out of the car and waited for Abel. The two of us, accompanied by a few other officers and SWAT team members, entered the area, which turned out to be an apartment complex.

"Did that paper list the apartment number?" Abel whispered as we crept into the complex. The interior suggested the building was running but it seemed vacant.

"It didn't say for sure, but 'D5' was separated on the note", I replied. I shined a light on some of the doors in front of us. "All of these rooms have the letter 'D' on them."

"Let's start searching. I want these assholes in my office by the end of the day," Abel declared.

The teamed scanned each door before I coincidentally found room D5. Interestingly enough, D5 was at the end of the hallway, about ten doors down from D1. I banged on the door.

"Chicago PD," I shouted. No one replied at the sound of my voice. The SWAT team headed in my direction with their weapons aimed at the door. Abel posted himself on side of the door.

"Julie Wilson?" an officer shouted, crouched in the far left. There was no response.

At that point, my anxiety heightened. My heart accelerated to the point where I felt breathless. I was frightened at the idea of it bursting out my chest.

'Do it,' Abel mouthed.

The SWAT team used the battering ram and knocked the door down. "Chicago PD, get on the ground," the team shouted as the officers entered the apartment.

I walked through the apartment clenching my gun.

"Clear!" SWAT members shouted as they looked inside of the various rooms.

"Looks like they're not here," I said as I continued to look around. Suddenly, a phone next to the living room TV began to ring.

"Don't answer that," Abel said. We all stood still until the answering machine got the call.

The person on the other line only breathed heavily.

"The fuck?" Abel whispered.

The person hung up, ending the recording.

Suddenly, I heard a car drive up outside. It slowed down but continued to drive once the driver noticed the police vehicles.

"This doesn't change anything," he said as he cleared his throat. "Keep this at the top priority. I want them in my office."

"Hubbard to Roberts," Jared said over his radio.

Abel grabbed his radio. "Roberts, here. Go ahead."

Jared continued, "suspicious vehicle is passing by. I'm going to light it up and pull it over."

"Proceed with caution," Abel said as he closed the snap on his holster for his gun.

I exited the building and made my way out front. I came just in time to see Jared turn on his siren lights and get behind the parked vehicle. He got out of the car and slowly approached walked the rolled-down tinted window.

"Is there a problem, Officer?" Michael said with a smile.

"Ah, shit," an annoyed Julie began in the passenger seat, "it's the cop from yesterday who keeps harassing me."

"Nice to see you both," Jared said. "Will you all please step out of the vehicle?" Jared put his left hand on his gun and spoke on the radio. "Julie and Michael are outside. I'm having them step out of the vehicle."

Michael opened the car door and stepped out; Julie did the same.

"What is it now?" Julie asked out of disgust.

"Julie Wilson, Michael Wilson, you are being detained and will be taken down to the station for questioning."

"Questioning for what?" Julie shouted. "We didn't do shit," she argued as an officer placed her in handcuffs.

"Julie, calm down," Michael said as Jared placed the handcuffs on him.

"What is this regarding?" Julie yelled.

"The robbery of the Ester Communion Bank and the explosion at your residence last night."

The team came out of the building and walked to Jared.

"Wait... our home exploded?" Michael asked.

"You're expecting me to believe that you didn't know that your home was demolished, between last night and this afternoon?" Jared asked as he walked Michael over to his car.

"Well, we haven't been home since yesterday," Michael calmly spoke.

"So, Officer, when are you going to just admit that you have a crush on me?" Julie asked calmly.

"Don't flatter yourself, Ms. Wilson," Jared stated as the officer put Julie in the back of the police car.

"The other officers are still inside," I spoke to Jared as she walked over to him.

"I'm going to drive these two down to the station and start this questioning. Have you heard from Richard?" he asked.

"Not a word yet. I was going to see how he was doing once we got these two," she nodded her head towards the car.

Jared shook my hand.

"Give Richard my warmest regards when you go."

"I'm not going just yet. Let's get these two down to the station and question them, especially about last night. Could have killed us all."

"Let's do it," Jared spoke.

6

-Linda

"About last night," Jared spoke inside of the interview room with Michael, Julie, and me.

"What about last night?" Michael asked.

I folded my arms and stood against the wall.

"Your home exploded and almost killed law enforcement," Jared declared. "And to make it worse, they found a camera that was transmitting the event over an internet connection."

"I told you before, Officer", Michael said, "we weren't home yesterday. We were on the road going to Wisconsin for business."

"Can anyone attest to that?" I asked.

"If you're not including the officer that pulled us over on the way to Wisconsin, then no."

"Do you know the officer's name?" Jared asked.

"Officer Johnson, I believe," Julie spoke. "White guy," she added.

Abel tapped on the window, alerting Jared and me to exit the room.

"Status, Roberts?" Jared asked as he approached him.

"DNA came back. It was a hit on Michael Wilson," Abel confirmed.

"So, it's living proof that he was involved in the robbery?" I questioned.

"For now, yes," he removed his hands from his pockets. "We're still trying to locate the helicopter that was used in the robbery. Without that, we're at another halt."

"We got Michael," Jared spoke. "So, we're not completely stuck."

"That's true. Go on and book him for being an accomplice to the robbery. We don't have anything on Julie, but let's take this one day at a time. This case could go on for longer than you think."

Jared and I returned into the room.

"That DNA sample we collected," Jared stated, "is a direct match. Congratulations, Michael, you're going away for being an accomplice to a robbery."

"Won't hold me for long. My lawyer should have me out of here in no time," Michael stated with confidence. "I know because I didn't do anything wrong."

"You sure about that?" Madeline asked as she entered the room with an envelope.

"Ooh, a cute lady cop," Michael spoke. "What's your name, cutie?"

"Officer Madeline Tucker," she laid the envelope on the table and took the contents out. "Here, we have a direct match to your DNA and the hair found at the scene."

"You know, you have some beautiful eyes," Michael flirted, ignoring her statements that proved he was in trouble.

"Now, all we have to do is match you up to the helicopter," Madeline hinted. "See," she showed him another picture, "the camera was able to catch the VIN of the helicopter. Now, you can help us out and tell us where to find the chopper and confess to the crime, or it can end up a lot worse."

"Let's make a deal," Michael spoke. "You give me your number, and I'll tell you whatever it is that you may want to know."

I butted into the conversation.

"So, you're admitting to knowing something?" I asked.

"That's not what I'm saying at all," he replied as he focused his attention on me.

"So, what are you saying?" Jared asked.

"What I'm saying," Michael looked at Madeline, "is that if this beautiful lady would like some information, I could help her find out something."

"Where's the helicopter, Michael?" Jared asked as he grew irritated with Michael's game.

"Michael, you have a helicopter?" Julie asked him.

He and Julie chuckled.

"I wish I had a helicopter. I'd fly my ass out of this city. Y'all cops are really buggin' right now," Michael sat back in his chair.

"You think this is a game, huh?" I asked.

"I know it's not, but I find it amusing that instead of catching actual criminals, you all are here bothering me and my cousin."

Jared looked down at the papers and up at me. As he was about to speak, the door to the room opened.

"I know you all aren't in here questioning my clients without their lawyer present," a woman stated as she walked through the door. "Michael and Julie, you all don't have to say another word."

"I'm sorry. And you are?" I asked the lady.

"Attorney Lisa Watkins. I will be representing Michael and Julie Wilson."

"That's all well, but these two are not currently under arrest," Jared spoke as he rose to his feet.

"I believe you just stated that you charged me as being an accessory," Michael spoke.

"Officers, this must be some kind of amateur operation. Surely, you can't arrest my client under suspicions. The fact that you all found his hair at the scene simply implies that he was in the bank. He did tell you all that he was at the bank earlier in the day making transactions," Lisa adjusted her hair. "Have you all found the supposed helicopter that was used?"

"That's currently under investigation," Jared argued. "The hair alone with images is enough to place him at the scene during the robbery."

"And we will argue that the hair was planted by CPD to detain my clients and make an arrest. You all needed some suspects, so you were quick to grab at someone… anyone."

Jared looked at me, and I looked at Madeline.

Lisa chuckled.

"Take a look at my 100% success rate. You have no case at the moment. Once you all get ahold of the supposed helicopter used in the crime or even the getaway vehicle, then we can talk. Until then, I see no reason for my clients to be held a second longer."

Julie and Michael looked at each other.

"Come on, you all," Lisa spoke.

"Once we find the helicopter, we will see you all right back here," Madeline argued.

"Good luck finding something that doesn't exist," Julie spoke.

"All aircrafts are traceable. Trust me, we'll find it."

"And the getaway vehicle?"

"If that's what it takes, we'll get that too," Jared spoke.

"You all are cute," Lisa spoke. "Give me a call once you have a real case."

Lisa handed Linda her card.

Julie, Michael, and Lisa all walked towards the exit of the interview room.

"What now?" Jared asked as the door closed.

"Well, I'm going to go to the hospital and check on Richard. Give me a moment to clear my mind."

"Shit!" Jared shouted. "Just like that, the damn case slipped through our fingers."

"Let's be patient," Madeline spoke. "Let's find that helicopter and van… and let's keep an eye on those two."

"When they slip up, we want to come crashing down on them like the walls of Jericho," Abel spoke through the door. "You three, take the rest of the day off. We need fresh minds on this case. We'll keep looking for the helicopter and van, and that's a priority. I'll see you all bright and early tomorrow."

7

-Linda

I left the police station in disbelief. Julie and Michael were roaming the town free and every lead my team collected got wiped. I arrived at the hospital and just sat in the parking lot. Scrolling through my phone, thoughts of the incident from the night before came to me.

I looked up from my phone and spotted Julie, Michael, and Lisa walking in the hospital.

Shit, they're here for Richard.

I sprung out of the car and bolted for the entrance. Fidgeting with my cellphone, I dialed Jared.
"Speak on it," Jared answered.
"J, where are you?" I demanded an answer.

"Heading home," Jared said. "I just left the station. What's going—."

I interrupted, "Meet me at the hospital. Julie and Michael arrived and walked inside. Without a doubt, they're heading for Richard's room." I stood out front waiting on Jared's response, looking through the glass to get an eye on the now three suspects.

I heard a car swerve on the phone. Jared grew loud. "On my way. Don't approach them, Linda. We can't have them claiming harassment."

"On it," I replied as I entered the building.

I hung up the phone and saw Lisa sitting in a chair. Julie and Michael walked towards the back. I approached the receptionist.

"May I help you?" the receptionist said.

I pulled out my badge.

"Hi, I'm Officer Linda Jackson. I'm here to see Detective Richard Young."

"Your relationship to the patient?" the receptionist asked as she typed on the computer.

"Friend and co-worker," I replied as I scanned the waiting room.

The receptionist handed me a badge and directed me to have a seat. "He's just returning from surgery. A party is heading to his room right now. Please have a seat and wait for clearance."

"What party entered the room, ma'am?" I asked growing nervous.

The receptionist looked at the clipboard and answered. "Julie and Michael Wilson. Friends of Detective Young."

Shit, no.

I held up my police badge while passing the desk. "Sorry, ma'am, but I'm going back there."

The receptionist detached herself from the desk. "Officer Jackson, wait until the other party leaves. You're going to get me in trouble."

I ignored the orders and bolted for the back.

A large security guard soon stopped me.

He took one step towards me. "Miss, you cannot see the patient while someone is already visiting."

I took one step closer. "If you don't let me back there, that patient, my friend, won't see the next day."

"Are you threatening the patient?" the guard asked. He used his large frame to almost push me back. I nudged back and pulled out my badge.

"Linda Jackson, C.P.D. I'm saving the patient from a threat. The individuals back there are main suspects of an ongoing investigation over the Ester Communion Bank robbery."

"We have another guard keeping an eye on the patient", the security guard said. "If anything goes wrong, they'll sound the alarm."

Disappointed and realizing there was no way I could get physically past the security guard, I turned around and returned to the waiting room. I sat next to Lisa. She didn't look in my direction, with her head in her magazine, but she spoke to me.

"Officer," Lisa began, smiling as she turned the page to the magazine, "what is it about my clients that gives you such a thrill?"

"Your clients are guilty; you and I both know it," I insisted.

Lisa chuckled, "It's not about whether or not we know. It's about producing evidence to convict them. You may think you have all of the evidence in the world," she looked at me, "but my 100% success rating easily proves that there's never enough."

I pulled out my phone but continued to speak to Lisa.

"...Besides, until you can generate evidence to connect them to the crime... You can't make them do the time."

I rolled my eyes. "If all of the evidence speaks for itself, there is no need to 'generate' anything."

"We will just have to wait and see, won't we?" Lisa smirked. "My clients aren't in police custody, because we all know the current case isn't strong enough for trial."

I leaned towards her. "We're working around the clock, so don't think we won't find enough evidence to finally put the criminals behind bars."

Lisa rolled her eyes. "Yes, the criminals... not my clients."

"What are they paying you?" I asked. "It amazes me how you defend them like they're not guilty. Must be a large check."

Lisa chuckled; this time louder. "Why ask such a thing? Officer, we both know the truth, but you won't side with my clients because it's your job to attack them. I wouldn't defend them if I felt they weren't innocent. The amounts I charge and am receiving are confidential. But I appreciate your curiosity."

Moments of silence passed, apart from the hospital intercom paging doctors and nurses. Jared rushed into the hospital and approached me. I rose to my feet before speaking to him in a whisper.

"How is he?" Jared asked.

"I couldn't head back there," I said. "Julie and Michael haven't left."

Alarmed, Jared turned away from me, sprinting for the patient area. Without hesitation, the receptionist jumped in front of her desk. I could tell she was prepared for Jared after dealing with me.

"Sir, you cannot go back there without checking in first" the receptionist yelled.

Jared took a step back. "Okay, may I have a pass," he asked.

The receptionist eyed him before returning behind her desk. Jared walked towards the desk.

"Patient's name?" The receptionist said, preparing to type.

Jared took out his badge. "Officer Hubbard," Jared said. "I'm looking for a Detective Richard Young."

"As I've explained to your partner," the receptionist began, pointing in my direction with her nail, "there are already parties back there. They have to exit before anyone else can enter."

Jared reached over the counter and snatched a pass, before swatting a folder of papers on the floor.

"I'm going back there," Jared stated while rushing to the back.

I wasn't expecting Jared to swipe a badge, but I knew that was my cue to follow him.

"They want to play, well let's play," Jared said as I finally caught up to him. We couldn't slow down because the security was dispatched. There was no turning back.

We rushed inside the room with Julie and Michael sitting on opposite sides of Richard's sleeping body.

"Chicago P-D," I shouted as I drew my weapon. Michael and Julie placed their hands in the air.

"Damn, baby," Michael said putting his hands up. "No need to announce that, we know who you are."

"Don't shoot," Julie said with a chuckle. She turned to Michael. "It's hands up... right?"

"Real cute," Jared said as he stepped into the room with his weapon drawn. He gestured for Julie and Michael to back away from Richard.

Julie and Michael looked at us in shock.

"I didn't realize that visiting a patient in the hospital was a crime, Mike," Julie said.

"I never said you were under arrest," I rebutted.

I never took my hands off of my gun or my eyes from Julie or Michael.

"Why don't you just lower the gun?" Michael said in a mockingly calm voice.

"Shut up," Jared said, holding his gun at Michael.

"We're here for the same reason you are," Michael said. "We just came to check on Richard."

"You came to check on a law enforcement personnel who is considering you to be suspect number one in a robbery? Try again," I replied.

We all walked back to the hospital's lobby, with the suspects in front of us. Once in the lobby, Lisa rushed to Julie and Michael's side.

"Do we have to press charges?" Lisa asked her clients. "I sense police brutality or harassment."

"No, Lisa," Michael said, "it's all good. Officer Jackson just has a misunderstanding of the situation."

"I really didn't think we were doing anything wrong by coming to the hospital," Julie said.

I stared at Julie and Michael. "You all can leave now," I replied while rolling my eyes.

"Let's go," Lisa said. "Apparently, coming to the hospital is a crime, and I'd hate to press harassment charges against Chicago P-D."

Lisa, Julie, and Michael left the hospital.

Jared watched the three leave while I returned to the room and noticed Richard opening his eyes.

"Welcome back to reality," I said entering the room.

Richard chuckled. "Thanks. I'm feeling a little sore," he replied. "But you know me, I'll survive it. What's happened with the case?"

"We're at a standstill," I said. "We did match Michael's DNA to the hair found at the scene, but their lawyer has already poked holes in our defense."

"So, we need to present a stronger case," Richard spoke as he tried to sit up in the bed.

"Easier said than done," I said as I walked over to assist him in sitting up. Jared finally arrived.

"Hey, my man!" Jared exclaimed. "We're ready to lock away those bastards now. Did you tell him about the DNA match yet, Linda?"

"Yeah, I did," I replied.

"I wish I could leave this hospital bed," Richard said as he shook his head.

"Do you know about how long you'll have to be here?" Jared asked.

"You'd be better off asking a blind man how you look," I chuckled at Jared. "The man just came back to reality."

"Doc didn't say. He said soon, but I'll need to use crutches for a few months. Perfect timing, right?" Richard said as he rolled his eyes at my joke and his current situation.

"Can we place the blame on them for the explosion?" Jared asked.

"Not quite. No fingerprints, no real clues that state that they planted the explosive."

"Julie and Michael are smart," Richard said. "Look at the bank robbery. Everything was planned to the 'T'. The only real pieces of evidence are the images that were taken by the roof-top camera and the hair left at the scene."

"What about a line-up?" Jared asked. "We never thought about bringing in the witness to identify them."

"That won't even be 100% accurate because the bank's tellers didn't see the criminals without the mask and disguises," I replied.

"It's a start," Richard said. "Let's get back to the scene of the crime and get the manager as well as any tellers who were present. Once we get the witnesses, let's get Julie and Michael back down to the station for a line-up."

"Not even 45 minutes out of surgery, and you're already talking about the next move. You are one determined police officer," I chuckled.

"Loss of life almost occurred. These two are on my shit list," Richard said with a slight laugh.

"Well, the moment you feel better, let's go get them," Jared said as he looked out the window.

"No, we do this now," Richard started to stand and I took one of his arms to assist him.

"You're in no condition to leave this hospital," Jared said as he took the opposing arm.

"This needs to be done," Richard replied. "One police officer being out doesn't mean the force stops."

Jared and I walked Richard over to his coat and he reached into his pocket. He pulled out his phone and began scrolling through it.

"No missed calls or anything," Richard said. "Jared, I want for you and Linda to go back out to the bank and bring the manager and tellers back to the station for a statement." We walked Richard back over to the bed.

"Need anything before we get out of here?" I asked as he got back in the bed.

"Nah, I should be set. All I can do is wait for these doctors to let me go," he answered.

"Well, we're going to get out of here and head over to this bank," Jared spoke. "Think you'll be home soon?"

"As soon as they give me the green light, I'll give someone the call. Oh, and make sure you all stay out of the crosshairs of Julie and Michael until it's time to bring them in for the line-up."

"Yes, sir," I replied.

I gave Richard a hug and Jared gave him a handshake. We left the room and walked down the corridor towards the exit.

"Think this is it?" I asked Jared.

"No. Julie and Michael will be back," Jared said. "I can feel it. I just don't want for them to start doing crazy shit and start trying to kill us."

"You really think they'll go that far to try to kill a cop?" I asked.

"People are crazy these days," Jared said as he pulled out his sunglasses.

"Nice doing business with you," Jared spoke to the receptionist as we walked past her.

The receptionist rolled her eyes at Jared.

Jared and I got into our respective vehicles and drove to the bank. During the drive, I couldn't get my mind off the amount of money that was stolen from the bank.

Nearly 3 million dollars. How the hell did they do this? That's more than what I would make in over a decade of working.

Jared and I arrived at the bank. The bank was still closed to the public due to the robbery. Construction work was being done to repair the damages caused.

Jared and I both got out of our cars. "Alright, Linda," Jared said, "pull out your badge. If they're smart, they will have beefed up security since the robbery."

"Well, they're familiar with my face since I was here with Richard. Let me lead and do all the talking," I pulled out my badge as we walked inside.

"Jennifer Lawrence?" I called out. Jennifer walked to the front to greet us.

"Nice to see you, Officer. How may I help you today?" Jennifer asked with a smile.

"Miss Lawrence," I began, "this is my partner Detective Hubbard. He's assisting the case along with Detective Young."

"It is nice to meet you," Jennifer said as she reached for a handshake from Jared.

"The pleasure's all mine," Jared responded.

"We're here to ask if you and a few other tellers would be able to come down to the station to help identify the criminals in a line-up," I added.

"Even though they were wearing masks and we didn't have a clear identification of them?"

"Surely, they must have spoken to you or had something that made them stand out in the crowd," I looked around the bank at the damaged pillars and glass on the floor.

"Detectives, surely if you have 20 people in the line-up that are wearing the same thing and look exactly alike, it will be hard to pick one out."

"All we're asking for is for you to come and do your best. If you don't wish to, we can't force you," Jared began, "but we have to inform you that without your cooperation, we won't have much success in catching these criminals."

Jennifer thought for a moment before speaking.

"Where's Detective Young?" Jennifer asked.

"Last night, there was an explosion at the residence of who we think was responsible for robbing your bank," I replied.

"Oh my," Jennifer said. "Is he...."

"Miraculously, no. Thank God," I responded. "He's in the hospital right now. But he may be on crutches for a while."

"He should be back on the case soon," Jared cleared his throat. "But for now, Officer Jackson and I would like to get you all to come and just attempt to identify these individuals in a line-up."

Jennifer started to give in.

"Is the identification today?" she asked.

"Well, it won't be today. We have to first get them back to the station to participate."

"Well, let me know when, and I'm sure it's something we can make happen," Jennifer asked.

"Let me ask you this," Jared said. "Is there anything about these individuals that stood out to you: whether it was the way they were built, the getaway car that was driven, phrases they may have spoken, the way they acted?"

Jennifer began to walk back towards the service desk of the bank; Jared and I followed.

"I know for a fact that it was a man and a woman," Jennifer spoke as she looked under the desk. "The woman did the robbery and the man drove the car straight through here and out the front door." She pointed to where the car drove and exited. "However, as the lady got in the car, she shouted, 'nice doing business with you,' before shouting something to the driver and he drove away."

"Are you able to recall what she said to the driver?" I asked her as Jared took notes on his phone.

"Honestly, I couldn't be too sure," Jennifer stated. "Looks like they were close, though."

"Miss Lawrence, are there any tellers here that would be able to identify these two in a lineup?"

"You mean besides the ones who were crouched for their lives behind these desks?" Jennifer chuckled. "Son of a bitch started shooting before she started talking. She was trigger happy," Jennifer spoke. "But she did grab one teller and hold the gun to her head as an intimidation tactic."

"Is she here today?" Jared asked.

"I believe she is. Let me radio her," she spoke. Jennifer pulled out a 2-way radio and spoke into it.

"Cassie Bryant, please come to the front."

While Jared and I waited, I noticed Lisa driving slowly by the bank.

I copied her license plate number down and stored it in my phone.

But she didn't slow down and looked like she had two passengers in the car. Jared pulled out his phone and scrolled to a picture of Lisa.

"Miss Lawrence, have you ever seen this woman?" Jared showed Jennifer the picture.

"Lisa Watkins," Jennifer stated without hesitation.

"So, you do know her?" I asked as I continued to scroll through images on my phone.

"Know her? I hired her." Jennifer spoke as she walked around the desk and crossed her arms. "She was a wonderful worker, but there was always a sneaky side to her. I know some people are quiet but damn. She was quiet, smart, and devious as shit."

"What about these two?" I asked her as I showed an image of Julie and Michael side by side.

"I've seen them in the bank before. I thought they were just customers here. But I don't know who those people are, no," Jennifer added.

"Why do you say that Lisa was sneaky?" Jared asked.

"She was one of those people that felt as though she could do something and talk her way out of it. For example, one day she came from the room with the safety deposit boxes and had many keys in her pockets. Now, there wasn't any money found on her, but she listed out this story about why she had the keys and how we couldn't fire her for it because of probable cause and if fired, she'd file for unemployment, and blah, blah, blah," Jennifer rolled her eyes at the end of her sentence. "She was honestly crazy."

Jared and I both gave each other a look.

"Yes, ma'am, you call for me?" a lady approached us.

"Cassie, this is Officer Jackson and Detective Hubbard. They're working the case of the robbery."

"Nice to meet you both," Cassie spoke.

"How are you doing, Cassie?" I asked her as I extended my hand for a shake.

"Recovering," Cassie chuckled as she shook my hand. "You try having an AK-47 aimed at your head with a lady shouting in your ear. The thing is, I know I could have whooped her ass if she didn't have that gun."

"And we're glad that you didn't," Jared answered. "For you to just stand there and let her scream at you, and to not react, took a lot of courage."

"Courage, my ass" Cassie rejected. The real courage would have been in stopping her from robbing us north of two million dollars."

"What can you tell us about the lady who came in and held you at gunpoint?"

"I was so close to her, I could honestly probably tell you the perfume she was wearing," Cassie let out a slight chuckle. "The woman had blue eyes. Not a deep blue, but medium tint."

"This is great," I typed what Cassie was saying into my phone.

"Medium length hair. Only reason I know that is because some of it was sticking out the side of her bodysuit."

Cassie tried her hardest to remember more about the lady.

"She wasn't that tall. Maybe a little taller than me... and I'm only 5'4. Can't tell you exactly how she sounded, because she was screaming the whole time she had me. It's honestly hard to identify a true voice that way."

"If you had to visualize the woman without the suit," Jared spoke, "would you say you've seen her before?"

Cassie popped her gum and put her hands on her head.

"If I had to say, I believe she's been in here before."

Jared excused himself from the group to use his phone.

"Cassie, we will need for you to come down to the station soon to identify the suspects in a police lineup," I told her.

"Officer," Cassie began, "you just tell me when you need me and I'll be there."

I reached into my wallet and pulled out a card. "Won't be today, but it will probably be within the next few days."

"We will be in touch," Jared said to Cassie as he returned. "That was Richard," he said. "They're about to let him leave so I'm going to head over there to pick him up."

"Detective Richard Young is also working the case," I told Cassie. "You'll meet him in a few days. You all have our cards and we know how to reach you. We needed to stop by and ensure that you all would be available to come and identify these individuals in a line-up."

"As I said, just let us know the day and time you need us," Jennifer spoke. "Send my wishes to Detective Young."

"You all have a good day," Jared spoke. "We'll let him know."

Jared and I walked away from the bank.

"Well, that was helpful," I spoke.

"Yea, now we just need to find about five other women with blue eyes that are about 5'5 or 5'6 with a close male accomplice."

"I'm sure that wouldn't be too hard," I laughed. "White women are typical, right?" I referenced his consistent jokes at white women and waved my finger in a circular motion towards Jared.

"You are something else," he mentioned as he got in his car.

"More than you'll ever know," I spoke in a low tone and started my vehicle.

I pulled out my phone and sent a text before Jared blew his horn to get my attention.

I deleted the text I sent and drove away with him.

8

-Richard

"Hello," I spoke as I answered my phone.

I finished buttoning up my shirt and made sure that everything was secure on me.

"Richard, how are you?" Abel spoke.

"I'm doing well; just waiting for these doctors to bring me these discharge papers so I can leave."

"What are they suggesting?"

"Well, I'm going to have to use crutches for a little while. Doc is giving me painkillers, but nothing that will prevent me from doing my job," I adjusted my gun in my holster as the nurse brought up my discharge papers. "Roberts, they're bringing me the papers, so let me call you once I get in the car."

"Sounds good," he stated before hanging up the phone.

"Alright, Mr. Young, the doctor says you need to use these for the next few weeks to two months," the nurse pointed to the crutches. "You will check in with us in the next month to give an update on your leg."

"What activities am I prohibited from? Anything that will prevent me from doing my job?"

"Try not to stand so much," she spoke. "We want your bones to heal and if they're constantly moving, it may be difficult for them to make a full recovery."

"Which greatly affects my job," I shook my head.

"We could provide a wheelchair for the next few weeks."

"No, that will handicap me even more. I can tough it out with the crutches, but I don't think I can promise you the thing about not standing."

"Detective, we can't ensure the proper healing if you aren't willing to take it easy."

"I'll be fine," I spoke. "I can promise to try to take it easy," I stated with a smile.

"Uh-huh," the nurse chuckled. "And these are the painkillers that the doctor is issuing," she handed me the prescription slip.

"These things are a definite way for me to sleep on the job." "Do us a favor," she spoke. "Don't. City needs you," she chuckled again. "Just take these if the pain becomes unbearable. However, you will need to take the antibiotics twice a day."

"I can do that," I replied. "Just can't have anything holding me back, you know?"

"I understand. Just ring for me when you're ready to leave out. I'll come to help you," the nurse spoke as she walked towards the door.

I texted Jared to ensure that he was at the hospital. I put my phone away and reached for the crutches.

"Guess I gotta get used to these," I thought aloud to myself.

My phone vibrated with a text from Jared; he was downstairs waiting for me. I pressed the button for the nurse and she came to my room.

"You ready?" she asked as she pushed in the wheelchair.

"Yes, I'm ready," I spoke. "But I won't be needing that chair," I spoke.

"You sure?" she asked.

"Yes. It will limit my mobility. I would just love your help in getting down to my ride," I chuckled. "We can put my stuff in the chair though," I pointed to my bag.

"I can help you with that," she smiled.

She lifted my bag and placed it in the wheelchair and we walked out of the room.

"I've heard a lot about you, Detective," she spoke.

"And what have you heard?" I asked her as I struggled to use the crutches.

She chuckled.

"Here, hold them like this," she adjusted my grip on the crutches. "And when you walk, keep your foot off of the ground and push up, using the crutch as your support system."

I took her advice and instantly felt a difference.

"You know your stuff, huh?" I chuckled. "Thanks."

"Well I am a trained nurse," she smiled. "But I've heard you're one hell of an officer."

"Where'd you hear that from?" I chuckled as we reached the elevator.

She smiled and rolled her eyes. "Are you trying to be funny?"

"Not at all," I humbled myself. "It's just crazy that you say that because I honestly wouldn't be anything without my team."

"A team player, I see," she spoke as the elevator traveled down to the lobby. "At least you can admit that you need others," she spoke.

"Well, what kind of man would I be to say that I didn't?"

"Wouldn't be much of one," she answered as we walked outside to Jared's car.

Jared opened his trunk and stepped out of the car.

"Stay off of your leg so much," she spoke. "If you don't, I will call your boss, personally, and request that he send you home without pay," she chuckled.

"You wouldn't dare," I chuckled as I put the crutches in the backseat.

She held my hand as I eased to the front door. I held onto the car as she opened the door.

I hugged her before sitting down.

"Thank you," I spoke. "I appreciate your help."

"No problem, Mr. Young. Check back in with me about your leg, soon."

"Will do."

Jared shook hands with the nurse before walking back to the driver's side.

"You ready, Mr. Smooth?" Jared chuckled.

I laughed.

"Yea, let's get out of here."

Jared left the hospital and drove onto the expressway.

"Did you all get the bank tellers to agree to participate in a line-up?" I asked.

"We got them," Jared spoke. "Once we get the line-up set, they're on board."

"Let's get that taken care of tomorrow, if possible," I chuckled.

"You don't waste any time, do you?" Jared asked.

"I'll sleep when I'm dead. Personally, I don't feel that I can rest until we put these two away."

"First thing is to get you home," Jared spoke. "You need some rest."

I looked out of the window as Jared drove.

Minutes later, he was arriving at my house.

"In all honesty, I think we can do the line-up the day after tomorrow. Tomorrow is a few hours away, and we need to get the suspects and everything else," Jared pulled out his phone.

"Damn," I shook my head. "Well if we're going to make a move two days from now, I guess I'll take tomorrow to myself and just 'rest'." I chuckled.

"You're a cripple now," Jared laughed, "you need some help getting in the house, old man?" he asked.

"Yeah, ok," I laughed. "Nah, I can do this."

I opened my door and got the crutches out of the backseat. I put my bag across my back.

"Keep me posted with what happens tomorrow," I spoke as I closed the door and walked to my porch.

"Will do," Jared shouted from the car window.

I unlocked the door and walked inside; Jared drove off.

I walked over to the kitchen and disarmed my alarm before grabbing a bottle of water and putting it in the bag.

I managed to get up the stairs with the crutches and walked to my bed. I put the bag down and grabbed the television remote off of the stand.

"And in other news, two suspects have been apprehended in the robbery of the Ester Communion Bank. Julie and Michael Wilson, ages 24 and 25, of the Flossmoor area, were detained earlier this week for questioning about the robbery. Once released from being detained, there was an explosion later that evening; injuring Detective Richard Young of the 26th District police department. They were then arrested again in connection to the robberies and explosion. However, due to a flaw in the 26th District's police department's evidence, the two have since been released and have personally reached out to Channel 7 news to tell their story, about the abuse they went through, while in custody."

"People really believe this dumb shit?" I thought aloud as Julie and Michael came on screen.

"...And I asked him why we were being detained, and they gave the response that we already knew the answer. So, you know, I'm just thinking 'something bad is about to happen in this station'. Not from our end, but I felt the officers were going to do something to us. And so, Detective Young and Detective Hubbard just kept getting louder and louder; screaming at us, calling us derogatory terms, and making us out to be these criminals that we weren't," Julie spoke.

"At one point, I could have sworn I saw Young reach for his gun. I was fearing for our lives and..." Michael added.

The camera switched back to the news reporter in the studio.

"Now, the police department has yet to release a statement on this situation. As you know, Detective Richard Young is one of the well-known officers in the community. Contact with him has been attempted but has not been established."

I muted the television and opened the bottle of water and took the antibiotic prescribed, as well as the pain killers.

"They put anything on the news, now," I spoke as my phone rang.

"Hello?" I answered.

Jared immediately started laughing.

"Do you see what these fools are trying to pull on us?" he asked.

"Hopefully Abel is smart enough to not fall for the fuckery they're doing," I chuckled.

"You resting?" he asked as he changed the subject.

"Trying to until I saw this crap. I just took these pain killers and antibiotics."

"Yea, well you need to get better," I could hear Jared's floor creak as he stood up.

"At least we know they're still in the city and aren't trying to run. Let them have their fun; they won't be laughing when we shut their asses down." I spoke. "But let me let you go. I'm probably about to take my crippled ass to sleep. I just did the dumbest shit though," I laughed as I thought of the situation.

"What's that?" Jared asked.

"I came up the stairs with the crutches, but getting down is going to be a bitch," I laughed.

"You got this," he joked. "Call me if you need anything, bro. You know I got you."

"Will do. Thanks," I hung up the phone and closed my eyes.

***

As the next morning came, I stood up and used the crutches as I walked over to the mirror.

"Look at yourself," I spoke. "Just a week ago, you were on top of the world, now you're at the bottom," I chuckled at the sight of myself.

My phone rang, interrupting my thoughts.

I walked over to it and answered.

"Hello?" I answered.

"Yo," Jared spoke, "you feeling better?" he asked.

"Yea, I'm feeling fine. Just throwing myself a pity party," I joked.

"Nah, don't even start," he spoke. "Gonna mess around and put yourself in your feelings and that's not what you need. That's not what any of us need," Jared laughed.

"Fuck you," I laughed. "What's up?"

"I'm just fuckin' with you. Nah, but I'm down here trying to get a few things done to get these suspects ready for a line-up."

"Get the other participants for the line-up first. We need people who fit the profile. I'm going to get off of my low horse and get to work researching if these 2 have access to a helicopter."

"Cool, cool. So, what specifically should we be looking for when profiling suspects for the line-up? Anything in particular?"

"You know: they have to be White and possibly working in a team. How tall is Julie? About 5'6-ish?"

"Yes sir."

"Okay, what about Michael?"

"He's about 5'9," Jared spoke.

"So, we're looking for 5'6 Caucasian females and about 5'9 males. It shouldn't be too hard to find people with police history and that fit the motive." I looked at the television.

"Any inner connections we should be looking for?" Jared asked.

"No. Let's focus on outer connections for now. I'm sure we have some suspects within the station who have been brought in on burglary charges."

"Okay. Well, I'll begin the search. You better be rested by tomorrow," Jared joked. "I'll be at your place at 7 o'clock on the dot."

"Don't worry about me," I laughed. "I'm always on my game."

"Yeah, you better be," Jared hung up.

"This nigga," I chuckled as I hung up the phone.

***

Jared and Linda both sat in their respective vehicles as they waited outside of Julie and Michael's hangout location.

"So, how do you want to do this?" Jared asked her.

"Well, we know what it is that we have to do," Linda answered, "but I think we should just tell them that something new has broken in the case and we need for them to come down to the station for a line-up."

"You think Richard has gotten anywhere in terms of finding information on the helicopter used?" Jared asked.

"If he hasn't, I wouldn't be mad. He's injured so I just want him to get plenty of rest. We will need him tomorrow."

"Yea, well that's true," Jared agreed as he put down his communication radio.

"All units, be advised, we have reports of a domestic dispute in the 3600 block of Fullerton."

"Mobile to base, mobile to base, shots fired at the 'Gold Lion Hotel & Casino'. Calling all available units to assist with the situation."

"A fire has broken out in the trailer park of the Addison neighborhood. Requesting a few units to investigate the cause as the fire department battles the blaze."

The radio began to send multiple transmissions to the officers.

"Should we go?" Linda asked.

"I'm not moving from this spot until it's time to get these two. You hear the transmissions are still going through." Jared turned off his engine and sat in the car.

"This is Unit 4343 alongside Unit 4039, we are sitting outside of the residence of Julie and Michael Wilson, waiting on the pickup to bring them back to the station. We cannot report to any of the disturbances at the moment."

Seconds passed before another transmission came through.

"Unit 4039, confirm your position," the lady spoke over the radio.

"Are they serious?" Jared chuckled. "Do they not trust my word?" he spoke.

"Unit 4039 awaiting suspect pickup," Linda spoke.

"10-4."

Jared didn't have to speak for Linda to tell that he was offended.

"Don't even take it personally," she joked as seconds passed and he hadn't said a word.

"They don't even trust me," Jared spoke.

"Suck it up," Linda joked. "Let's just wait and get these two."

Jared and Linda both stepped out of their vehicles and Jared walked over to Linda's car.

"So, how long do you think these two are going to stay in the house?" he asked as he leaned on Linda's car.

"As long as it takes. They already know that they're suspects and we're going to be returning to them for a line-up," Linda spoke.

"What makes you say that?" Jared asked.

"Remember, I'm White," Linda chuckled.

"Well, that's a good enough reason," he joked as he put his hand on his gun, which resided on his side in the holster. "Let's just go inside and get these two."

"I'm right behind you," Linda spoke as they walked into the building.

They walked to the apartment of Julie and Michael and slowly knocked.

"Julie Wilson, it's Linda Jackson from the Chicago Police Department."

There was no answer; just the soft sound of music emitting from the room beyond the door.

Jared tried to twist the knob; no luck.

"Should we kick it in?" he whispered.

"Let me try to knock again, first," Linda replied as she knocked. "Julie Wilson," she spoke louder.

No answer.

Jared shot at the hinges of the door, kicked in the door, and aimed his gun. Julie and Michael were sitting on the couch in the living room; right behind the door.

They instantly put their hands up.

"What the hell?" Julie shouted as she was startled.

"Stand up," Jared spoke to Julie and Michael.

As they rose to their feet, Linda put them both in handcuffs.

"Look at this, Linda," Jared stated as he looked at the laptop they were working on.

"You can't look at that," Julie shouted.

"Julie, calm down," Michael calmly spoke to his cousin.

Linda walked over to the laptop as she finished locking the handcuffs.

"Looks to me like they're breaking into something," Linda spoke.

"Look here," Jared began as he pointed to lines of text on the screen. "Fire at Addison trailer park, shots fired at Gold Lion, violent acts in the 3600 Fullerton area... Either they were listening in to the transmissions, or those transmissions weren't real."

"Yea, and look at this," Linda pointed to another window that opened to her touch.

"Blueprints of the Ester Communion Bank and side notes..." Jared spoke.

"You can't fuckin' go through my computer," Julie argued.

"Same things a typical hacker could gain access to," Jared argued. "Look at this note, Linda. 'Be sure to leave no evidence and destroy...'" Jared chuckled. "Seems like these two made sure not to put any self-incriminating evidence here."

"Where's the helicopter, Michael?" Linda asked as she walked them over to the door.

"I have no idea as to what you're talking about," he smirked.

"You all are under arrest," Jared spoke as he and Linda walked Julie and Michael out of the room and downstairs.

"Just don't say anything until we call Lisa, Julie," Michael spoke.

"This is unit 4343 returning to base. We have suspects Michael and Julie Wilson in custody," Jared spoke over the radio.

Jared and Linda both drove to the police station, and upon arriving, they walked Julie and Michael inside.

"I knew it wouldn't be long before we had you all back in here," Jared began as he and Linda put Julie and Michael into the cell. "Especially after you all fabricated that story and put it on the news."

They didn't say a word.

Lisa walked into the building.

"I hope I'm not too late," she spoke.

"You know, I wish I could say I was surprised to see you here," Linda rolled her eyes.

"Well, the news reported that you had my clients in custody, yet again."

"Can't touch them right now," Jared spoke. "Tomorrow they are in a police lineup involving the robbery."

"Do you all always go above and beyond like this? Or is it because my clients are White?"

"Out of options, so you have to play the race card, huh? I hope that's not your defense," Linda chuckled. "You must not realize that I'm White myself."

"This has nothing to do with race," Jared laughed. "Besides, your clients have ultimately admitted guilt."

Lisa looked at Julie and Michael.

"Never store evidence against yourself in a computer or anywhere online." Jared continued.

Lisa smirked. "Did you two have a search warrant for that evidence inside of the computer?"

"Didn't need one," Linda spoke. "It was out in plain view during this arrest."

"Until you all pull valid information with a valid warrant, that information is null and void, and not applicable to the case."

"Well, we shall let that be until we find that helicopter they destroyed," Jared chuckled again.

"You really think you've won, don't you?" Lisa questioned.

Jared and Linda looked at her.

"Where's your boss? I would like to speak with him."

"I'll radio him and find his location," Linda smiled.

"Jackson to Roberts," she spoke over the walkie-talkie.

"Roberts here," he radioed back.

"Requesting your location as a lawyer would like to speak with you on behalf of Julie Wilson and Michael Wilson."

"Returning to base," he began. "Those transmissions that were sent out were all false."

Linda and Jared looked at each other, before looking and Michael and Julie.

"I think I know how that happened. What's your ETA?"

"About 5 to 10," he replied.

"10-4," Linda replied as she put the radio back on the desk.

"Good enough for you?" Jared asked.

"That's perfect," Lisa stated. "I guess I should just have a seat until he arrives?"

"Or you can stand if you want. It's your choice," Linda stated with a slight smile.

Lisa walked over to the chair next to Linda's desk and took a seat.

"When is this lineup supposed to take place?" Lisa asked as she messed with her phone.

"We're scheduling it for tomorrow," Jared spoke. "We have other suspects, in pairs, that fit the same motive… this way, your clients get a fair trial," Jared answered.

"If they supposedly didn't show their face, how can anyone point them out?" Lisa asked, never looking away from her phone.

"Don't worry about that. But if they are identified, and with the evidence we discovered today, please believe they will be locked away."

"Well you all can kiss that evidence goodbye," Lisa spoke as she looked up for the first time in minutes. "You can't obtain evidence by literally scrolling through someone's computer unless you have a search warrant."

Abel walked into the building and walked to his office.

"Is that your boss?" Lisa asked before Linda or Jared could reply to her comment.

"That's your guy," Jared replied as he dialed my number.

As I answered the phone, he excused himself from the room.

"Yo, Rick," he spoke.

"Yea, what's up?" I replied.

"You get anywhere on the search for that chopper?" he asked me.

"Did a little work on it, but I honestly haven't gotten anywhere with it. What's up? You have an update?"

"I got better than that," he began.

I heard his office door close.

"You remember the camera caught the VIN of the helicopter?"

"Yea, I remember that."

"Look for dumps and landfills and recycling centers that have recently received parts that may go on a helicopter."

"Why are we searching landfills and such? Shouldn't we just look where helicopters can be stored?"

"Well, you know that Linda and I went to apprehend Julie and Michael today," he began.

"Yea, I know," I answered.

"On the computer they were working on, it had a complete blueprint and plan on the bank, as well as a note that said, 'be sure to leave no evidence and destroy,' but then there was no more text," Jared spoke. "But I'm pretty sure they were going to mention a helicopter. Not to mention they hacked into the system and sent out false transmissions to distract the police."

"Well," I started as I sat up, "let's get to work. Tomorrow, I'll be good to go and we can get these two in the system."

"Yea, but you know that Lisa is already trying to say we can't use the evidence."

"Don't pay her any mind. Just let Roberts know what you found and run a trace on where those transmissions came from. If the result is an IP address, run a comparison to the IP provided by

Michael's Internet provider. If it's a match, we got them on that charge, to say the least."

"So, should I go by their home and retrieve the IP first or what?" Jared asked.

"No, the first step is to determine where those transmissions originated. The evidence is on their PC so make sure they can't access and delete it."

"I'll get right to it. Run a search on the VIN and determine if it has a last location, and if so, look for areas where they can dispose of the parts nearby."

"Okay, will do. But do not let them leave tonight, under any circumstances. If they leave tonight, we may not be able to find them by morning," I spoke.

"Nah, they aren't going anywhere," Jared answered.

Jared hung up the phone and left his office.

"Mam, I'm sure everything that Officer Jackson and Hubbard did was within protocol," Abel explained.

"What about the damage to my clients' property or searching through their computer without a warrant?" Lisa calmly asked.

Abel looked at Jared, then to Linda, and proceeded to speak to Lisa.

"The city will repair the door, I will see to it."

"And the computer?"

"Roberts, we didn't search the system as the data was on the screen. All we did was see it. We haven't logged it in, yet," Linda spoke.

"There's your answer. If you need us to, we will get a search warrant and we will search the computer thoroughly. But we will have it by morning, and you all aren't permitted to go near the system until we do." Abel spoke. "None of you," he reiterated to Julie, Michael, Jared, Linda, and Lisa.

"Your command has been received," Jared added.

"Is that all, Miss?" Abel asked.

"For now, I just have to accept it for what it is," Lisa spoke.

Lisa picked up her purse and put it around her shoulder. She walked over to the cell where Julie and Michael were.

"Okay, guys, I'm going to leave for the night. But what I need for you all to do is stick together. Do not speak to these officers or other inmates about anything. I will return here bright and early in the morning for the lineup. Honestly, you all don't have much to worry about."

"Thanks, Lisa," Michael replied.

"Jared, please escort Ms. Watkins downstairs. It's getting dark and we don't want her returning home so late." Abel spoke.

As Lisa walked, Jared followed behind her. All was silent until they arrived at the elevator.

"Office, let's be honest for a moment," Lisa spoke as they walked on the elevator.

"Okay, go for it," Jared replied.

Lisa pressed all of the numbers on the elevator so that she and Jared would have time to talk.

"Are you serious?" he asked her.

She ignored the question and continued.

"I can tell you and Richard are close."

"Yes, mam, that we are," Jared answered.

"This bond goes beyond work."

"What are you getting at?" Jared asked as the elevator stopped at each floor.

"I think this vendetta that you're feeling towards my clients, is because Richard is injured, and he's holding a vendetta."

"Miss Watkins," Jared started.

"Call me 'Lisa'," Lisa spoke.

"Lisa," Jared started again. "I can assure you that I'm just devoted to doing my job. Honestly, I have nothing against your clients, on a personal level. So, you can save your stories and assumption."

"If you say so," Lisa spoke as the elevator reached the final floor.

"You have a good night, Officer," she spoke as she walked off the elevator.

"You, too, Lisa," Jared spoke as the elevator closed.
***

Jared sat outside of my home the next morning awaiting my departure.

He beeped the horn even though he saw me exiting the home.

"If you blow that damn horn one more time," I shouted.

"Well bring your slow ass on," Jared joked.

I walked off of the porch and used the crutches to get to the car.

"Any longer, I would have been an old man," Jared joked as he pushed the car door open.

"Yea, whatever," I chuckled. "Just wait till I'm off these things."

"You'll still be an old man," Jared laughed.

"You got jokes, huh?" I responded. "Anyway, is everything set?" I asked as I abruptly changed topics.

"Yes sir, we're all good to go. Julie and Michael are sitting in a cell and you already know that Lisa is there bright and early."

"That should be good news. What about the witnesses?" I asked.

"Linda and another officer are heading back to the station with them right now. You know Lisa called herself having a discussion with me yesterday, right?"

I laughed.

"What could you all possibly have to talk about?"

"Basically, she told me that the reason I was out to get Julie and Michael, was because you had a vendetta." Jared shook his head.

"That's funny to me," I spoke. "Question is, why is she so adamant that the two are innocent?"

"They could be related to her," he suggested.

"Something's going on," I spoke. "Seems a little suspicious to me. What about the warrant?"

"Abel has just gotten one, so we should be good to go with that. He is sending a unit over to get the laptop."

"So, we really should be all set to go," I answered.

"Let's just hope the witnesses pick these two out in the line-up."

"We both can tell that they're guilty, so it really shouldn't be an issue," I spoke to Jared as he pulled into the parking lot.

We both got out of the car and walked inside the station. As we walked onto the elevator, Lisa followed.

"Detective!" she exclaimed as she looked at the crutches. "You're back."

"Yes, mam. Couldn't stay down for too long," I replied.

"Well, it's good to see that you're doing better, although you are on crutches."

"Crutches or no crutches, someone's gotta do the job. Don't worry about me because I'm going to do the best I can, regardless," I looked at Jared.

"I spoke with your partner last night," Lisa spoke, changing the subject. "It's quite a vendetta you all have with my clients."'

"It's like I told you yesterday, there is no vendetta," Jared spoke. "We're here to bring justice to the table and leave our personal biases at home."

"Is that really what you're doing?" Lisa chuckled. "Seems a little fishy to me, but alrighty."

The elevator lifted to the top floor and the door opened.

Lisa was the first to exit the elevator and walked over to the cell that held Julie and Michael.

"Welcome back," Abel spoke as he shook my hand.

He looked at the crutches.

"Guess you have to tone it down a bit, huh?" he asked.

"I mean, I can't run a marathon, but I'm committed," I laughed. "I'll get the job done, Roberts."

"That's exactly what I like to hear," he spoke. "Commitment."

An officer walked off of the elevator holding the laptop and Linda brought in some papers.

"You got the witness?" I asked her.

"They're waiting in the room. Don't want these criminals to intimidate them." She handed Jared the paperwork. "Glad to see you're back on your three legs," she joked.

"Everybody got jokes about this, huh?" I chuckled. "It's okay; I'll be back to myself soon."

"You know we're just messing with you, Rick," Jared spoke. "What are these for, Linda?"

"Gotta go through and get these verified and signed after the line-up. There are a few we need to get the witnesses to sign as well." Linda looked towards the cell and made eye contact with both Michael and Julie.

"Well, let's get to it," Jared spoke.

I used the crutches and walked over to the line-up room alongside Jared. As we walked in, I shook hands with the witnesses.

"Detective Young, it's so good to see that you're doing much better," Jennifer spoke.

"Glad to be doing better. Thank you," I told her.

"This is Cassie Bryant, Detective. She's one of our tellers and was held at gunpoint by the suspect. She'll be helping with the line-up."

"Very nice to meet you, Ms. Bryant," I spoke.

"Nice to meet you as well," she replied.

"Miss Bryant, we will need for you to fill out this form for the line-up," Jared spoke as he passed her a piece of paper. "It's a confidentiality agreement and states that you are doing this on your own will and haven't been promised any compensation or bribed into participating in today's line-up."

"Seems simple," Cassie spoke as she signed the paper.

I used the crutch and flipped on an additional light switch.

"Now, Cassie, this is a one-way mirror. Meaning that you will be able to see and identify the suspects and distinguish between who's who, but on their side, they will be looking in a mirror," I explained.

"So, you're positive they won't be able to see me?"

"1000% positive," Jared spoke. Can't hear us either unless we have the mic armed."

"I'm not even going to lie to you all," Cassie spoke. "I'm a little nervous."

"That's understandable," I spoke. "Just take your time and do your best. We'll be right here to aid you with whatever."

Ten minutes later, Abel walked into the room with the DA and Lisa. The suspects walked into the adjoining room. The women were first.

"Cassie, do you see the woman who was holding you at gunpoint?" I asked her.

She looked closely.

"Take your time," Jared spoke.

"Can you have them speak?" Cassie asked.

"Masks on and say the phrase provided, in the tone asked," Jared spoke over the mic.

The women put on the masks and each took turns speaking.

"Keep your head down and let's empty the backroom. You do that, you go home for dinner tonight; understood?" each of the 6 women shouted.

"Can you have number 3 repeat it?" Cassie asked. "I'm sorry."

"It's no issue at all," I spoke. "Number 3, please repeat the phrase without modifying your pitch or tone."

Woman 3, who was Julie, repeated the phrase.

"That's her!" Cassie exclaimed. "That's the woman who held the gun to my head."

"Are you sure?" I asked her.

"Yes. I'm positive. That isn't something that I would forget."

"Bring in the male group," Jared spoke after he tapped three times on the glass.

The group of men walked into the room.

"Now this will be tougher," I spoke. "They will put on masks but they won't say anything as the male didn't speak during the robbery.

"Masks on," Jared spoke.

Each of the men put on their mask and Cassie looked at them.

"Take your time," I spoke.

"I can't identify him," she spoke after a few minutes of silence.

"You sure?" I asked her.

"I didn't get a good enough look at him to identify him."

"Take them out," Jared spoke over the mic.

"Thank you, Cassie. You did good," I told her.

"So, what's going to happen next?" she asked. "I wasn't able to identify the male."

"Well," I began, "with your help, we are now able to convict the woman. Don't worry too much about the male. It's not your fault. He stayed in the vehicle and you didn't get a good look at him."

"Your identity will remain confidential and the suspects will never know who identified them." Jared walked towards the door.

"Detective," Jennifer spoke. "If anything comes up, be sure to give me a call," she finished.

"Will do. Keep your head up during this rebuilding process, and if you need anything from us, personally, don't hesitate to give me a call."

"Thank you," she spoke.

An officer escorted Jennifer and Cassie out of the room through the back so that there was no chance of them being seen by the suspects.

"Well, I guess that we got Julie as actually being a part of the robbery," Jared spoke with relief.

"Yea, but what about Michael?" I asked.

"We got his hair to place him there," Jared replied. "Let's take it step-by-step. This is a break that we've been looking for."

"Let's keep our fingers crossed," I spoke as we left the room.

9

"How does it feel to have been in this cell for the last month and a half?" I asked Julie as I walked over to her cell.

"Well, I can't say much. I know that I didn't commit the crime, and I believe your witness may have made a mistake," Julie replied as she sat on the bed reading her book.

"You know, we can cut you some kind of deal with a confession and if you lead us to the money."

"Why would I confess to something that I didn't do? That would be stupid," Julie chuckled.

"Have it your way," I replied as I continued past her cell.

Julie kept her eyes on me as I walked to the elevator with Jared.

The holding cells were in the basement of the station and my office was on the 7th floor.

Jared and I exited the elevator and walked to my office.

"So, what have we got?" I asked him.

"They've finished searching the computer. Using that, they think they've come closer to finding the helicopter," Jared spoke.

"Have we run a check on their bank accounts for the past few months? See if there's been any abnormal spending that could point to money being spent on a helicopter."

"The largest transaction on Julie's account was for a purchase to Amazon in the amount of $679.87."

"Can you pull up the account in here?" I asked him. "I want to keep a close eye on it."

"I'm sure that we can get some officers to pull it up," Jared spoke as he walked over to the window.

My office phone rang and I answered on the first ring.

"Detective Young?" an officer asked over the speakerphone.

"Speaking."

"This is Officer Brown. I'm giving you a call about the account you have us watching, belonging to Julie Wilson."

"Okay, what about it?" I asked.

"A deposit of $5000 has just posted to her account."

I gave Jared a look as to say 'really, nigga?'.

"Impossible. She and her cousin are both sitting in a cell awaiting trial. Do me a favor and find out the list of authorized users on her account. If that's money from the Ester Communion bank, we have her. Have there been any other postings?"

I could hear the officer typing to pull the list for me.

"About a week ago, there was a deposit of ten thousand."

"We got her," I spoke as I rose out of my feet. "Pull that list for me," I spoke to Officer Brown before hanging up.

"Plans?" Jared asked.

"I have plans," I chuckled. "I will be asking Julie about this, with you alongside, but then I'll be leaving here and heading to that bank."

"Fifteen thousand in a matter of 2 weeks. Damn, I wish I was banking like that," Jared joked. "You sure you don't want assistance in going to that bank? You know we haven't heard from Linda, so I gotta watch your back." Jared made sure that his holster was secure and walked to the door.

"Yeah, I know. I've been calling but to no avail. I hope she's doing alright. It's not like her to flake on us, especially during a break in the case."

I locked my computer and left the desk lamp on. I made sure my gun was secure in the holster and dialed Linda's number again from the office.

It rang seven times before going to voicemail.

"Hey, this is Linda Jackson. I'm sorry I'm not able to come to my phone right now... Just a bit. On any note, please leave a message with your name and number and I'll give you a call back at my earliest convenience." Her voice went off and the tone chimed.

I didn't leave a message.

I picked up the receiver and put it back down to hang up the speaker.

"You know what, I may drive by her place once I leave the bank. Meet me there when I give the call?" I asked Jared as I rose to my feet.

"You know I got you," he spoke.

"My dog," I spoke as I shook his hand and gave a one-armed hug.

We both left my office and returned to the lower level.

"Richard! Jared! We never see you all just causally down here," the guard stated as I signed our names on the clipboard.

"Something has come up," Jared spoke.

"We need to see Julie and Michael Wilson." I scratched my soul patch and the officer put out a transmission to bring Julie and Michael to the room.

We removed our guns from the holsters and placed them on the counter.

There was a loud buzz and I knew it meant Julie and Michael were in the room.

"Richard," the guard spoke. "Behave yourself this time."
***

About eight weeks ago, I'd completely lost my temper when a snotty drug dealer wouldn't talk about his stash. Instead, he tried to play me for stupid.

As I asked him where the drugs and guns were, he insisted that they were 'from my Uncle and he'd know exactly where they were'. I had to chuckle at the foolishness and I reached over and grabbed the man by his collar.

"You must not know who I am," I told him. "I'm your worst fucking nightmare," I shouted in his face.

"You're a funny one," he chuckled.

I slammed my hand on the table, startling him and the guards.

The guards quickly rose and ran over to the room. They grabbed me as I shoved him to the floor.

"Young, that's enough," a guard told me as he held me.

"Police brutality?" the drug dealer asked as he was helped to his feet.

"You don't know brutality," I spoke.

***

"Julie, Michael," Jared took a seat in the chair across from the two.

"Yes, officer?" Julie spoke.

"Who's depositing into your account?" I asked, still standing.

"Why, what ever do you mean?" Julie asked in a mimicking tone.

"$5000 was posted to your account less than an hour ago. And you're in this cell so there's no way you could have done it yourself," Jared put the piece of paper on the table in front of Julie and Michael, which was their bank account summary.

"You all are watching my account?" she asked. "I hope you all have a warrant for this."

"We have exactly what we need. Plus," Jared sat up in his chair. "You're both in jail for the robbery of the bank. We have the right to watch your account for unusual activity."

"And what would you consider to be unusual?" Michael asked.

"How about a deposit of $10,000 last week?" I interjected. "What about $5000 moments ago?"

"Let's not forget to mention that the $5000 was posted to your account while you're in jail," Jared added.

"Direct deposit," Julie immediately retorted.

"I guess we'll find out soon enough, although your statement doesn't state that it's a direct deposit."

"No offense, officers, but if you have what you need, why are you down here talking to us?" Michael asked.

"Don't be a smart ass," I spoke as I kept my arms folded across my chest.

"On the contrary," he added. "I'm just asking a genuine question. Instead of focusing on us so much, you all should be tryin' to find the actual criminals." Michael sat back in the chair and gave me a devious look.

"15,000 in less than a month. I wish I had that much to deposit in under a month," Jared joked. "You guys know you're on my boy's shit list, right?"

"That's what you want to say?" Julie asked. "Aren't these rooms tapped?"

I looked at Jared as he looked towards Julie and Michael.

Michael and Julie gave satisfied looks as I checked the time on my phone.

"Let's go, J," I spoke as he rose out of his chair.

"No more questions?" Michael asked. "We were just getting to the fun."

"No questions, but I have a statement," I replied as I turned around. "Since you all don't want to be cooperative, once the bank tells us who's authorized to make deposits on your account, the DA is not going to try to make any deals with you."

Jared and I left the room before either Julie or Michael had the opportunity to reply.

"So, what's next?" Jared asked.

"Well, I'm going to head over to the bank and check on these deposits. Julie and Michael don't want to be cooperative, so we gotta handle this ourselves. And once I leave the bank, I'd like for you to meet me at Linda's."

"I got you. Just give me details."

"As soon as I leave the bank, I'll call you and we'll agree on a meet-up point."

"That sounds like a plan," Jared spoke.

We shook hands and I pulled the keys out of my pocket; I walked out of the station and walked over to the police vehicle.

On the ride to the bank, I decided to give Linda another call; maybe she'd answer this time.

To no avail, I ended the call and continued the drive to the bank.

***

I left the bank without any success, so I called Jared.

"Speak on it," Jared answered.

"No luck," I replied. "Saying I need to physically bring in a warrant to authorize the release of documentation."

"Well, I'll inform Abel and he can start the process of getting the warrant."

"Sounds like a plan. Meet me over here at the bank with my car. I miss my baby," I joked as I sat in the police vehicle.

Jared laughed at my comment.

"Don't you have your keys?" he asked.

"I keep a spare set in the office," I answered.

"I'm on my way," Jared hung up the phone and I returned the phone to my pocket.

I closed my eyes and decided to rest as I waited for Jared.

Moments later, the smell of gasoline interrupted my rest, so I decided to roll down the windows.

The petrifying odor continued to grow stronger and was soon at a point that I could no longer tolerate it.

I stepped on the accelerator instead of the brake, accidentally, and the engine began to smoke.

I turned the car off and quickly got out of the vehicle. I got as far away as I could.

Pedestrians were walking past the vehicle and stopped to look at the emerging smoke.

"Chicago Police Department, step away from the vehicle!" I shouted toward them.

As the pedestrians began to scurry away, the vehicle exploded.

"Someone call 911," I shouted as I ran towards the vehicle and pedestrians.

"Detective Young; reporting from CCB Bank. A police vehicle exploded and we have civilians down. Requesting many buses and cars," I shouted over the radio.

"10-4," Isabella replied as she repeated the transmission.

As people continued to scream and run, I attempted to get the crowd under control, but I knew I wouldn't have much luck being as though I was the only officer at the scene.

I ran over to a woman on the ground, screaming in pain.

"Ma'am, my name is Detective Young, I'm from the Chicago Police Department," I spoke to her calmly.

"It hurts," she cried softly as she began to calm down.

"I'm going to assist you in whatever way I can, and there are ambulances on their way. What's your name?"

"Lucy Castonelle," she spoke.

"Tell me where it hurts," I told her

"My right leg, near my thigh."

Ouch! Just hearing about her pain in her leg made my leg tingle.

"Can you move it at all?" I asked her.

"It hurts if I even attempt to move it."

"Need those buses, where are they?" I asked over the radio.

"About 5 minutes out," Abel spoke over the device.

"They will be here soon. Keep your leg relaxed and just keep talking to me," I spoke as I tried to keep her calm.

As she spoke, Jared drifted around the corner and came to an abrupt stop next to the burning vehicle. He got out of his car with his gun in his hand.

"Over here, J," I shouted.

He trotted over to the lady and me.

"What the hell happened here?" he asked as people continued to run around him.

Businesses began to close their doors to stop people from entering.

"Jared, this is Miss Castonelle. I'm believing that my car had a gas leak and as a result, it exploded. Ms. Castonelle was in the proximity of the explosion and has gotten injured."

"The ambulance is right around the corner," Jared spoke as he saw her holding her leg. "The pain is in your leg?" he asked her.

"Yes," she spoke.

"What have you all done for it, Richard?"

"We haven't done anything. I had her attempt to move it, but nothing more than massage it and apply pressure to it." I replied.

The sound of sirens quickly filled the streets as ambulances, fire trucks, and police vehicles all came speeding down the street.

The firetruck came to an abrupt stop as the officers also stopped. One of the ambulances drove to the end of the street and one stopped right beside me.

"Ms. Castonelle, I'm going to leave you in this paramedic's hands as I go and check in with the other officers," I rose to my feet.

"Thank you for all of your help, Detective Young," she stated.

"It was absolutely no issue," I smiled as I walked away.

Firemen were watering down the vehicle that I was driving to wash away the flames.

"Detective, you might wanna have a look at this," the lead fireman spoke minutes after they extinguished the flames.

I walked over the burned pieces of metal towards the leader.

"What's going on?"

"Do you know the cause of this explosion?"

"I'm assuming there was a gas leak. I started smelling it, and as the odor grew and I couldn't stand to be in the car with the odor, I got away from it."

"Your gas line was cut," Abel explained. "This was no wear and tear."

"Are you sure?" I asked.

"I've been doing this for years," he chuckled. "And seeing as though you didn't smell the leak when you left the station, I'd say that this line was recently cut."

"I don't believe this shit," I spoke, disgustedly. "Can you get any evidence of who may be responsible?"

"I'd recommend you get forensics over here. They will have much more success with those things," the fireman spoke.

"Well, let's get them over here. If someone just tried to kill me and has a beef with me, I want for them to face me the best way I know."

I walked closer to the car and looked at the gas line.

Forensics specialists came over and began to dust the gas line of the vehicle.

"We got prints," the lady shouted.

"Can't wait to pull these results so I can get whoever's responsible for this," I thought aloud as I touched my soul patch.

The forensics specialist ran the fingerprints through her machine and it began to scan the database for matches.

"Think Julie or Michael could have been responsible?" Jared walked up beside me.

"Come on. Even they don't have the necessities to pull this off," I retorted.

"You'd be surprised," Jared replied. "Think about it. They planted a bomb in their own house to try to kill you... I wouldn't put this past them."

"I suppose that it's possible. We'll have an answer soon enough. Everyone's prints are stored in a system."

"We've got it," the forensics' officer spoke.

"So quick?" I asked.

"There's a large number of databases that the system could possibly pull from. How'd you all pick the right one to start?"

"We started with the most common: the police database. During the scan, it scans the employees first, inmates second."

"And with the results coming back so quickly..." Jared started.

"One of our own fucking men tried to kill me," I shook my head, angrily.

"Try women," the officer added.

"The fuck?" I asked.

"Officer Linda Jackson," she showed me her computer screen.

"Wow. So, I'm assuming this is why we haven't heard from her. She's fucking scheming."

Anger was emitting through my words.

"Nah, there has to be a logical explanation. She couldn't have done this," I denied. "Can you dust for more prints?"

"We can try," the lady spoke. "But we can't swear that there will be any more hits."

"Just try it, for me. Please," I spoke as I turned to Jared.

"What do you want to do?" he asked.

"I guess we wait. I would have never thought that Linda would be the one behind this. I guess you're right," I chuckled and lowered my voice to a whisper, "white women are crazy."

Jared laughed.

"You a fool," Jared watched the forensics officer's computer screen and looked at Linda's image. "That's a damn shame."

"I wonder how Abel will respond when he finds out,"

"He will most likely have the same reaction that we're having. Honestly wouldn't have expected Linda to be the one to do us dirty," Jared hung his head.

I continued to scan the screen with the program, praying for a new result.

"Lord knows I don't want to have to bust Linda," I spoke aloud.

The system displayed the same image of Linda with the words 'scan completed'.

"I guess this does explain why we haven't seen her," Jared replied.

Abel drove up beside us and emerged from his vehicle.

"Give me the details, Young," he spoke as he made sure his gun was holstered away.

"Gas line was cut while I was inside of the bank, and because of this, the car exploded. Luckily, there's only one injury, but I think she'll be fine. I'm gonna go check on her and see how things are looking."

"Any prints from forensics?"

"You're not gonna believe this shit," Jared spoke.

"Why?" Abel raised one of his eyebrows.

"Linda," I spoke. "That's why."

Abel shook his head in disgust. "Explains why we haven't heard from her."

I could tell Abel was in disbelief.

"Fuck," he spoke softly.

"I'm gonna go check on Lucy," I spoke as I walked away.

My thoughts were racing as I kept picturing the image of Linda on the computer screen.

"How is she?" I asked the paramedic.

"She'll be just fine. Just a little minor bruising, but nothing to be too concerned about. She'll be on her feet in no time," the paramedic applied a bit of pressure to her wound.

Lucy lied on the gurney and looked at me.

"One beneficial thing was that she was calm. So, her vitals were good and we didn't have to do much in that respect."

"It's all in a days' work," I spoke.

"She's a tough one," the paramedic spoke. "I typically experience patients with broken bones or internal bleeding after an explosion, but not Ms. Castonelle," he chuckled.

I smiled at her.

"You know I have to thank you," she spoke.

"Thank me for what?" I asked.

"Why else do you think my vitals are so good?"

"You have the heart of a bull," I joked.

"It's all because of you," she chuckled, "and I greatly appreciate that."

"Just doing my job," I put my hands in my pocket. "I have to get back over with the other officers, but I just wanted to make sure you were doing alright," I spoke.

"So kind," she chuckled. "Thanks for coming back over."

I proceeded to walk back over to Jared and Abel; thoughts of Linda swarmed my mind.

"How's she doing?" Jared asked.

"She's doing fine. Just a little minor bruising. What else have you all come up with?" I asked.

"Well," Abel started, "DNA isn't wrong, and Linda's is definitely all over your gas line."

"Yeah, she didn't give your shit any chance at life," Jared chuckled. "Don't fuck with them White women."

"It's something wrong with you," I laughed. "Nah, but seriously, just thinking about Linda doing this has my head all messed up."

"I wonder where she is now," Jared thought aloud.

"Do we have to suspend her account from the system as of now?" I asked Abel.

"I'd have to check. I believe we revoke her privileges until we catch up with her. Remember, everyone's innocent until proven guilty."

I walked over to my vehicle and sat inside the driver's seat.

Jared walked to the passenger's seat and opened the door.

"How the hell am I just supposed to let Linda go like that?" I asked Jared. "That's been my partner for so long, and my friend for even longer than that."

"She's no good for you or the squad. Clearly, she doesn't care. She just tried to kill your ass," Jared chuckled. "Fuck her, you don't need her anyway. She was holding you back."

"I guess that I can look at it that way," I spoke. "But it's still hard."

"Nah, I can completely understand, bro. You know I'm here regardless of what happens."

"I respect that about you," I replied as I reclined my chair.

"I'm gonna step back out for a second," Jared replied. "Gonna figure out what Roberts wants us to do."

"Hopefully it's not too much," I joked, yet had a slight hint of seriousness.

Jared stepped out of the vehicle and I turned the volume up slightly.

I let the words of Eminem speak my thoughts.

Friends are people that you think are your friends
But they really your enemies, with secret identities
and disguises, to hide they true colors
So just when you think you close enough to be brothers

Abel interrupted my thoughts with a tap on the window. I opened my eyes and rolled down my window.

"What's up?" I asked.

"While me and a few other officers finish cleaning this mess, I want you and Jared to head over to Linda's place and see if she's there. If she is, bring her down to the station for questioning regarding this explosion and see if she's working with Julie."

"We can do that," I spoke. "Shouldn't be too hard to track her down."

"If she isn't home, make sure you check her hangout spots, favorite places to eat..."

"Abel, I got this," I chuckled as Jared got into the passenger side of my car.

Abel let out a chuckle and tapped the side of my door twice before I drove off.

I had to give complete focus as to what was about to happen, so I turned the volume all the way down for the entire drive.

***

"Linda?" I called as I knocked on her door.

"Shit, she may not be home," Jared spoke as he held his gun. "I don't see her car."

"Yeah, you're right," I spoke as I removed my gun from the holster. I took a look through the small spacing of the wooden planks of Linda's gate.

"Linda!" I shouted as I saw her running through the yard. "We got a runner," I spoke excitedly to Jared.

I threw my body into the gate and it swung open.

I returned my gun to the holster and proceeded to chase behind Linda.

Jared followed me on the pursuit.

"Linda, stop," I shouted as she started to climb down the mirroring side of the fence.

I threw my body into the fence she was on, and she fell back.

Linda rose to her feet and continued to run.

I hopped the fence and continued to chase her as Jared did the same.

Linda ran into the street in an attempt to lose us.

Cars began to swerve to avoid hitting her. Many drivers came to an immediate halt as she held her hand up while running through traffic.

"Shit's not worth it, Linda," I shouted as the cars almost hit her.

"Fuck off, Richard," she spoke as she ran around the cars and through the outside strip mall.

"Watch out," she spoke as she ran into some of the customers.

She knocked over merchandise from the street merchants in an attempt to slow Jared and me down.

"Destruction of property, assault, evading police; got this bitch," Jared shouted as he ran behind me.

Linda ran through the store and back onto the main road.

"Linda, watch out," I shouted as a car almost hit her.

She jumped to the right and moved out of the way before the vehicle collided with her.

She continued the chase into the forest that resided nearby.

"Come on, J," I spoke to Jared as we ran around the cars.

We ran into the forest and began to look around; we didn't see Linda anywhere in sight.

"Fuck," I spoke out of disgust.

"White girls can run," Jared joked. "Plus, she probably knows these woods inside and out. She lives right behind it."

Jared and I heard a splash and ran to where the sound originated.

We came to a river and scanned it for Linda; no luck.

"She's gone," I spoke as I shook my head.

"How the hell did she disappear so quickly?" Jared asked.

I ignored his question and proceeded.

"You ready to go back to the station and get our asses handed to us?"

"Shit, we may as well," he chuckled.

We began to walk back to my vehicle and my cellphone rang.

"Young speaking," I answered.

"Hey Richard," the woman spoke.

"Julie?" I asked.

"You didn't recognize the number to your own police station?"

"It's pretty funny that you've decided to waste your phone call on calling me," I chuckled.

"Why'd you say that?" she chuckled.

"Your little friend," I started, "just led us on a chase through her hood," I stated as I controlled my breathing.

"I don't have friends, only family," Julie remarked

"That's what you have, huh?" I asked. "Well, your 'family' just bolted like a bat out of hell when she saw me."

"Who are you talking about?" Julie asked.

"The one who switched sides to work with you; you know exactly who I'm talking about."

"Damn, I haven't the slightest clue as to who you could be referring to," Julie chuckled. "Rich, I gotta go."

Julie hurried off the phone.

"Was that Julie?" Jared asked.

"How'd you guess?" I asked with a chuckle.

"It's a classic. White girl is on the run and all of a sudden, out of nowhere, you get this mysterious phone call from her partner in crime," Jared chuckled as secured his gun in his holster.

"Let's get the hell out of here," I uttered as we walked back over to my car.

I drove back to the police station: empty-handed and slightly disappointed.

"You two, bring your asses over here," Abel spoke.

"Damn," Jared whispered under his breath.

"What's the assignment?" Abel asked as he walked into his office.

"Roberts, we're attempting to apprehend Linda," I calmly replied.

"It seems like you all understand what needs to be done," he began.

He looked at Jared and back at me.

"So, where is she?" he continued.

Neither Jared nor I replied.

"I'm gonna take that as an 'I don't know'," Abel replied. "So, with that being said, all these calls I'm getting from civilians and pedestrians about a foot pursuit and destruction of property is for nothing."

"Cap, it's not for nothing," I replied.

"Yea, I mean, the bitch was right there. She just slipped through our fingers," Jared immediately answered.

Abel looked up at Jared almost immediately.

Abel swiveled around in his chair to his file cabinet. He pulled out a folder and turned back around to the desk. He opened the folder and laid out the images that resided within.

"These look familiar to you?" Abel asked.

I looked at the images.

"That's definitely Linda," I spoke.

"Looks like she's trying to fix something," Jared answered.

"These pictures were captured by surveillance cameras around this building. These were taken last week, so we have to ensure that every single car that's in our lot is inspected to ensure she hasn't sabotaged any other vehicles."

"So how exactly does this pertain to us?" Jared asked.

"That's where it gets interesting," Abel chuckled. "Seems like you all are passionate about getting your girl, so this is your shot. Linda's your assignment. I think the two of you should be able to apprehend one lady, am I right?"

Jared and I looked at each other.

"Here's the deal. Bring her in, but keep a low profile," Abel leaned over the table. "I don't want a single call to come in about anything that the two of you have done to apprehend her, and I don't want any reports from you until you either have her, or have a lead on her," he finished in a stern tone.

"You got it, Boss," Jared answered.

"Don't screw this up," Abel spoke as Jared and I rose to our feet.

"Already on it," I answered.

Jared exited Abel's office and I followed.

"So, we get the assignment of chasing the White girl," Jared asked as we walked outside.

"If you look at it from a different angle, it could be a simple solution. I mean, we've worked with Linda for years, so we know her habits."

"And what are you saying with that information?" he asked as we stood at my vehicle.

"I'm saying we know how stable she is. We know what to look for to apprehend her. We know what kind of cars she goes for, her hangout spots. Come on, bro. Think."

"So, what? You wanna stake out at her place?"

"Shit, unless you got a better idea," I unlocked the car door and got inside.

"And what happens if we see this bitch?" Jared asked through my window as he got into his vehicle. "You know Roberts said to keep a low profile."

"Just gotta get her, you know? By any means necessary," I started my engine.

"You love pissing him off, huh?" Jared chuckled.

"You know me," I joked.

10

"I spy, with my little eye..."

"Absolute bullshit," Jared replied with a laugh over his radio. "Man, we been out here for nearly twelve hours and haven't even gotten a hint of where this girl may be."

"We just have to wait it out," I answered. "She'll be back."

"She better hurry the hell up," he rebutted.

"This is shield 4352, reporting outside of suspect Jackson's home. No movement as of yet, just confirming the location," I spoke over the radio.

Jared sat in his vehicle across the street from where I was parked.

"Just stay vigilant," I spoke to Jared.

"I know a song that gets on everybody's nerves, everybody's nerves, everybody's nerves. I know a song that gets on everybody's nerves and this is how it goes..." Jared began to sing.

"Don't even start, before I turn your ass off," I spoke to Jared.

"It's just so damn boring sitting outside this woman's house," he replied.

I ignored his comment.

"Stay vigilant," I spoke to him. "I'm gonna rest my eyes for a second."

I closed my eyes; I was exhausted.

"Leave it to Abel to assign us to the bullshit assignment." I could hear the slight attitude in Jared's voice.

"That shit's gonna feel so good once we take her down. Woman tried to kill me," I chuckled. "I'm glad that it wasn't my car that she blew up."

Although I spoke to Jared, I kept my eyes closed.

"So, there's a chance that she didn't try to kill you. She was just trying to get *someone*," Jared added.

"The shit people will do for money," I replied. "Makes people even turn their back on their own family."

"It makes the world go around," he suggested.

"Look alive. We got a blue corvette coming down the street. Seems like the kind of car Linda would drive."

"Duck your head down and don't make any sudden movements or motions," Jared pressed record on his dashboard camera.

"Turning into Linda's lot," I spoke over the radio.

"You think this is her?" Jared asked.

"It may be," I kept my attention on the car.

The car turned off and Jared and I sat in silence as the person emerged from the vehicle.

"Lisa?" I spoke over the radio.

"What the hell?" Jared asked.

"What kinda shit is this?!"

"That ass is got," Jared spoke.

"Why else do you think Lisa'd be over here, unless Linda's guilty of something?" I asked as Lisa walked to the home and unlocked the door.

"Should we go get her right now?" Jared asked.

"Nah, let's wait a little while longer. Linda is our assignment, so that's where we keep our focus."

"I hate this part right here..." Jared started to sing.

"I hate you, J," I responded to him.

***

About three hours passed before there was any sign of movement.

"One rainbow... two rainbows..." Jared continued to utter random words, phrases, and lyrics into the radio to keep us 'entertained'.

"J, you've been doing this non-stop for the past 17 hours. I swear to God if you don't stop, they're going to have to send units over here to get me off of your ass," I stated with a chuckle, yet was serious.

"Man, we've been choked up in these cars for the longest, staking outside of this woman's crib. I stink, I'm tired, I'm hungry... help me, nigga!" Jared joked over the radio.

I couldn't hold in my laughter any longer.

Yes, Jared was being extremely annoying, but he was also keeping us both alert. I noticed Linda's door open and Lisa emerged.

"Alright J, straighten up," I reported. "We have movement outside of Linda's residence," I radioed the other officers.

"It's Lisa. Julie's lawyer."

"The hell is she doing over there?" Abel asked over the radio.

"Say the word: we'll bring her in," I replied.

"Go on and bring her in for questioning," Abel replied. "We got some information for you all to review anyway."

"I thought you didn't want to see us again until we apprehended Linda, Cap," Jared asked.

"Don't sass me, Hubbard," Abel replied sternly.

I pulled my badge from the glove compartment and stepped out of the vehicle. Jared emerged from his vehicle as well.

"Lisa Watkins?" I spoke aloud.

Lisa peeked over her shoulder.

"Detective Young, how nice to see you."

Lisa was completely unaware that we were on her trail.

"Lisa, we're going to have to ask for you to come with us," Jared mentioned as we approached her from two different directions; just in case she decided to try to run.

"Come with you where?" she asked as she stopped walking.

"Down to the station," I answered. "Perhaps you can answer the question as to why you're leaving Linda Jackson's home." I proceeded to walk behind her.

"Please put your hands behind your back," I uttered.

Lisa obeyed.

"You all have *got* to be kidding me," she replied. "So now it's illegal to visit a friend."

"Friend?" Jared asked. "Since when in the hell are the two of you friends?"

"We have similar interests," Lisa spoke. "I didn't realize it was illegal to make friends."

"It's not," I locked the handcuffs on her and walked her over to my car.

"You know, I think I'm going to sue you all for police harassment. Everywhere I turn, you all are there harassing me and my clients."

"Good thing you're a lawyer; that way, we don't have to appoint one for you."

I helped Lisa get into the backseat of the vehicle and closed the door.

"I'll get this situated before you can even count to 3."

"3," I immediately replied.

***

"Why were you at Linda's home?" I asked as Jared entered the interrogation room.

"That's not a crime, Detective," Lisa calmly replied. "If you can regulate who's home I can and can't visit, what's next? Are you gonna say that I can't wear lingerie unless I'm about to have sex?"

"Hah!" Jared exclaimed. "You make me laugh. Richard, you gotta get yourself one of these," he remarked.

"It's hard to tell if you're being serious," I replied. "Because, see, Linda's currently a wanted woman, and so it's not like you're just visiting a friend. You're visiting someone who contacted you because they wanted your legal services."

"You can prove this?" Lisa asked.

"What is it with this woman?" Jared asked. "Does she need for you to spell it out for her?"

"That would be nice if you can effectively list out the crime you all have me here on."

I cleared my throat.

"We don't have a crime on you, as of yet. But just watch your back." I lowered my tone. "Keep fuckin' with Linda, and you're gonna be caught up as an accomplice."

Abel tapped on the window three times; Jared and I stepped outside the room.

"Y'all get anything on her?" he asked.

Jared prepared himself to speak.

"Other than speculation?" he added.

Jared closed his mouth.

"We're working on it," I added. "But to be honest, the case won't be strong at all."

"With us holding her now, we're really just hoping she leads us to catch Linda."

"Exactly," Abel replied. "That leads to police harassment cases, and that's the last thing that this department needs." Abel adjusted his tie. "Cut her loose."

Jared looked at me.

"Now," Abel added.

I walked back into the room and Jared followed.

"Attorney Watkins... guess who's free to go," I announced.

She chuckled.

"I knew I would be sooner or later. I'm still thinking about pressing charges."

"Technically, we just said we were bringing you in for questioning," Jared spoke with his arms crossed as he leaned against the door.

"You're playing it smart, I see," Lisa spoke as she looked at the water in the cup. "You guys won't plant my DNA anywhere if I drink this, will you?" she asked with a smirk.

"Take the cup with you," I spoke. "We're not desperate for anything," I replied as she rose to her feet.

"I really hope you all find what you're looking for," she spoke as she took her keys from her purse.

Jared made a face at her as she left out the room.

"And just like that," Jared wound up his arm as if he were pitching for baseball, "that girl is outta here!"

"Man, shut up," I chuckled. "Let's go see what they want us to review. I'm ready to get to the heart of this case, to be honest."

Jared exited the room and I followed.

"We got so much shit we have to solve," Jared chuckled. "Linda trying to kill us; Lisa's collaborating with Linda, now; not to mention, all of this started over a robbery."

"Not just any robbery," I spoke. "They made off with north of two million. And not to mention, we can't find the damn chopper they used," I laughed as we approached the break room.

"My question is: how do you lose a helicopter? You know how big those things are?"

"Is everything a joke with you?" I laughed.

"As far as I see it, you gotta laugh in life or else it'll beat you down. Especially in the workplace."

"You're right about that," I added.

I didn't show it, but the stunt that Linda pulled, truly affected me. She'd been working with me for years, so for her to change sides for no apparent reason, it hit me as if it were a personal vendetta.

But I had to keep a straight face. I couldn't let personal problems come into my work, or else, my judgment would be clouded.

"Pretty soon, this will all be over," Jared remained optimistic.

"There you guys are," Madeline spoke as she entered the break room. "I think they've found out information about that chopper that was 'lost'."

"Why the air quotes around 'lost'?" I asked.

"You'll see," Madeline lifted an eyebrow as she walked into the adjacent room.

"This is so messed up," I chuckled as Jared and I followed Madeline.

"So, check it out, right? We ran the vehicle number that was captured by the surveillance cameras."

"And?"

"Is it stolen?" I asked.

"Stolen, no," Madeline stated. "But we can't quite find a direct owner." Madeline pulled out another document. "But when we ran the ID number, we were able to locate where it was purchased. 'Sky High Helis and Jets', it's a company based in Atlanta. So, what do police officers do when they find this information out? We research." Madeline pulled out another document.

"Damn, girl. You put your foot in your mouth with this research," Jared joked.

Madeline chuckled.

"So, what was your hit when you discovered the company? You find out who bought it?" I asked her.

"I called them, and the helicopter was purchased using a prepaid card. You know what that means."

"No name on the card," Jared chuckled. "Don't prepaid cards have limits on them?"

"Not those Visa cards. They paid over 20 thousand for the helicopter. But, they record ID numbers of everyone who makes purchases, so we're just waiting to get the number back from them."

"I know damn well if I pay that kinda dough for anything, there's no way I'll be wasting it. Especially not to use it in a damn robbery," Jared spoke.

"So, where do we come into play?" I asked.

"We're getting closer to solving this," Madeline answered. "We're just waiting to hear back from Visa regarding the sale. It had to originate from somewhere. We're looking into bank accounts of the suspects to see if any withdrawals were made around that amount."

"Lisa, Julie, Michael, and make sure you get Linda in that scrap."

"Just need for you all to hold put for a little while longer," she closed the folder. "As soon as we get the ID number, we can crack down on who purchased the helicopter, and have a new lead on this robbery."

"Young, Hubbard," Abel spoke as he entered the room. "Calumet City police have found what appears to be the remains of a helicopter. I want you two to head out there and take a look at the rubbish. Forensics already has a lead on you, but I want for you all to discover whatever they find."

Jared and I exited the police station and got into his assigned police vehicle.

"Aye, we can't have Madeline showing us up like that. Acting like she's top cop and shit," Jared joked. "That's our job."

We both sat down inside of the vehicle and Jared turned on the siren. He exited the parking lot and sped towards I-290.

"Why are you speeding, again?" I chuckled. "You know this isn't necessarily a crime."

"So, what, you're gonna complain about my driving too?" Jared asked as he approached an intersection.

"Nah, you're straight," I laughed.

My laugh was interrupted as a vehicle, whose driver wasn't listening and observing the overhead flashing lights, collided with our vehicle as he drove through the green light.

11

The siren died as the car crashed through the guardrail and flipped over onto the expressway.

I could hear cars blowing their horns and swerving to avoid colliding with us.

"Fuck!" I shouted as the car flipped right-side up. "You cool, J?" I asked him.

Jared didn't reply to me. Instead, I could see the anger in his eyes.

"It's a fuckin' shame when no one follows the rules of the road," he growled.

Jared ensured his gun was secure in his holster and attempted to open the door.

No luck.

"You good, bro?" Jared asked.

"I can hardly move," I spoke. "I can't feel my upper body."

"Hubbard to base. Two officers involved in a t-bone collision on I-290 east entrance by Pulaski. Multiple injuries and car is not drivable. Please send assistance."

By now, onlookers were causing a delay to see what was going on. Many people observed the accident and I could see that plenty had their camera phones out, but none came over to help. I'm assuming the civilians' first thought wasn't to assist the police with anything, especially with all that was going on.

"10-4. We have assistance in route to your location," Isabella spoke over the radio.

"Sit tight, bro," Jared spoke as he shot bullets through the windshield. He smashed what was remaining of the windshield with the butt of his gun.

Jared climbed through the open hole and stood erect.

I tried to reach for my phone while I waited. I could hardly move a muscle without feeling severe pain. As Jared stood at attention outside of the vehicle, I could see multiple scratches on his face. I looked up and saw part of a broken mirror. I caught a glimpse of my face. There were many cuts and abrasions, and a stream of blood ran down from the top of my head down to my lips.

"You good in there, B?" Jared called to me as he set the hazard cones from the trunk.

"I'm good," I called out. "I just wish this help would hurry the hell up. Keep an eye on the driver of the other vehicle. Go make sure they're good," I uttered.

An ambulance arrived at the scene and a car pulled up behind it.

A lady emerged from the vehicle and jogged over to the car.

"Oh my..." she began. "Let's get you out of here," she attempted to open the passenger door.

I immediately recognized her. It was the nurse that had helped me before when I was in the hospital.

"Mr. Young, can you hear me?" she called out.

"I can hear you," I managed to speak. "Now, just get me the hell out of here and we'll be good," I chuckled.

"Everything will be fine," she spoke.

I saw her smile, and it was enough to give me a little energy.

"When you all crashed and flipped, the car's doors caved in, so I'm going to ask for your help. Do you think you can climb through this windshield?"

"Honestly, I can barely move," I answered, weakly.

"I want for you to try, okay?" she asked. "For me?"

I managed to control the muscles in my hand to unbuckle my seatbelt. Although every bone in my torso was aching, I managed to lean forward and lift from the chair.

"That's it," she spoke as she reached her arms through the windshield.

She didn't care about the fact that she could severely injure herself in the rubble; her only concern was to get me out of the vehicle.

"Come on, baby," she spoke gently as she wrapped her arms around me and pulled me from the vehicle.

"Shit!" I shouted as she pulled me through the windshield.

She laid me on the gurney that the paramedics unloaded from the ambulance.

She put her jacket over me and held my hand as the paramedics lifted the stretcher.

"Richard, can you hear me okay?" he asked.

"Yes," I replied.

"Where are you feeling the most pain?" he asked.

"It's all over," I responded with an irritated tone.

"Miss, you have to step back," he announced.

"Nurse Madison Miller," she pulled out her ID. "I'm going to be riding with him."

I finally knew her name.

"Let's get him loaded onto the ambulance and to the hospital as quickly as possible," one of the paramedics spoke to the team.

They put the stretcher onto the ambulance and Jared came over.

"Find out how the hell this happened," I told him as I held Madison's hand. "I want their ass when I get back to the office."

"Shit, bro, I'm starting to think that you're like an injury magnet. You keep getting hurt," Jared chuckled.

I slightly shook my head. "Just do your job, bro," I chuckled.

"I'll be by there once we get this cleaned up."

The paramedic closed the ambulance door and drove off.

We sat in the back of the ambulance with a paramedic who monitored the fluids being pumped into my body. Moments of silence passed before I spoke.

"I'm starting to think you're my angel," I flirted with Madison.

"Oh yeah? Why's that?" she asked.

"This is the second time you've been to my rescue when I've been injured."

"Well, Richard," she began, "you know I'm a nurse and it's what I do," Madison chuckled.

"Don't be a smartass," I joked. "You know what I mean," I emitted a chuckle but felt a pain in my chest as I laughed.

"Just relax, Richard," she gently informed me. "Don't laugh or do anything strenuous."

I obeyed her commands and closed my eyes.

Just my luck.

Madison stroked my hand and I could hear the paramedics working to keep fluid flowing through my IV and keep my blood pressure steady.

I felt a kiss on my forehead and I opened my eyes.

The paramedics unloaded the gurney and wheeled me into the emergency room. They transferred me from the gurney onto the bed.

"Stats?" A doctor called out.

"Richard Young, 23 of the Chicago Police Department. He and his partner were riding to a crime scene when their vehicle was involved in a side-impact collision. The impact pushed the vehicle onto the I-290, where it flipped numerous times. His partner sustained minor injuries, such as scrapes and cuts."

"Alright, let's get him into a room and perform a cat-scan. Keep Mr. Young comfortable," the doctor spoke.

They wheeled me into the room for an emergency cat-scan, and once it was over, they wheeled me into another room and connected me to an IV machine to keep my body hydrated.

They connected me to a blood pressure monitor as well, but they had to place the cuff on my leg considering my torso was in pain and they didn't want to bruise me any more than I already was.

"This shit's unreal," I uttered as the nurse left the room.

They ensured that I kept my head elevated and cuffs on my calves to keep the blood circulating throughout my legs.

"What is?" Madeline chuckled as she sat up in the chair.

"I'm right back where I started. It may be worse this time," I knew that something was broken.

I emitted a small laugh.

"All I can think about is when that car hit us. It was almost as if it was a planned thing."

Thoughts of Julie and Michael ran through my mind. Had they known we were getting closer to solving the helicopter mystery?

"You know what I think?" Madison rose to her feet and picked up the container of apple juice.

She inserted the straw and took a sip of the drink. She walked over to the bed and sat on the edge.

"I think you need to relax," she whispered as she held the straw to my mouth.

I looked at her and sipped the drink.

"Tastes good, right?" she whispered.

"What's your deal?" I asked her with a laugh.

"What do you mean?" she replied with the question.

"You're so flirty with me this time out."

I enjoyed her flirting, but at the same time, amid everything that was going on, I was a little skeptical.

"You must not remember our last encounter," Madison chuckled. "You need to relax," she kissed me on the forehead.

Madison rose to her feet as one of the machines started to beep.

She walked over and pressed a button on the machine to silence the alarm.

"As your nurse for the evening," she joked. "I demand that you relax," she closed the door to my room.

I thought for a fact that she was going to try to do something sexual; but what good would I be? I was paralyzed for the moment and could barely control my muscles.

She pulled the chair closer to the bed and turned on the television.

"Let's try to get some sleep, Richard," she spoke before kissing me on my forehead.

She extended the chair to the lounge position and reached her hand over to hold mine.

"Good night, Madison," I spoke as I held her hand tightly.

∎∎∎

"Richard! You're back!" Abel spoke as I wheeled myself into the room.

"And looking a lot different," Isabella chuckled. "You sure you're ready to return to work?" she asked.

I laughed.

"Don't let this chair fool you. I'm only using it to get around the office. I'm not going to need this crap when I'm working these streets."

"We're not putting you back on the streets until you are healed," Abel spoke.

"Cap, I'm fine. I'm able to work."

"Nah, bro. We need some paperwork to prove you can return. You come wheelin' in here trying to take over," Jared joked.

"Yea, yea," I chuckled. "I'm assuming we haven't made any progress on that helicopter they said they found."

"Henry and I went over there, but when they scanned for prints and things of that nature, no luck."

"Alright, cool," I replied as I wheeled over to a table. "While we feel that we're in a slump, let's wait for that ID number from that Heli's and Jet's place. We keep doing what we do best until then."

I rolled my sleeves up.

"We police."

"You all heard the man," Jared announced after I finished speaking. "Let's get back to work."

Officers scattered about to their offices.

"Damn, man. It looks like you're running this joint. I know I definitely would think you're running the show around here and that you were more than a cop," Jared mentioned.

"Yeah, whatever," I replied. "So, what exactly happened with that helicopter?"

"I met forensics at the scene," he began, "but everything was torched. Pretty much impossible to get a hit on it. One thing I did see, was the ID of the helicopter. You know you can't eliminate those, no matter how hard you try."

"So, what'd you get?" I asked.

"It's the same chopper that was used in the robbery."

"Well, now we know where it went," I shook my head. "What about Linda? Do we have a tail on her?" I asked.

"We've had a few cars patrolling her area, but it hasn't been around the clock like you and I were patrolling."

"Figures," I chuckled. "No one gets shit done like the best in the force."

I shook hands with Jared.

"Enough about work," Jared spoke after shaking hands. "What's up with you and that hot nurse I've been seeing you with? You get it yet?" he joked.

"It's not even like that," I laughed. "But she truly has been a blessing. When I need something, she's there."

"What's her name, again?" Jared asked.

"Madison. She's pretty amazing," I answered.

Jared paused and looked at me.

"You got angel dust in your eyes," he chuckled.

"Man, shut up," I playfully hit him.

"Nah, man. You're in love."

"First things first," I spoke. "I don't fall in love. It does nothing to you except end in heartbreak and turmoil. Plus, it's way too soon to say I'm 'in love'. I'm just seeing what she's about," I spoke as I wheeled away towards my office.

"Uh-huh," he called out. "You can say what you want, but I know the truth," he chuckled.

"Stick to what you know, J," I raised my middle finger while entering my office.

Moments passed by and Jared walked into my office.

"What's good?" I asked as I put a folder into the filing cabinet.

"Call me crazy, but hear me out," Jared put his hands in his pockets as he began to pace the floor.

"What kind of crazy shit are you plotting now?" I chuckled.

Jared grabbed a dry erase marker and walked towards the board.

"So, you got Michael, Julie, and Linda as our three suspects right now."

"For the robbery?" I asked.

"In general, but let's throw Linda into the robbery as the inside/outside man... or woman, in this case."

"Uh-huh," I spoke.

"You got a torched helicopter and a deposit totaling 15K in under a month into Julie and Michael's joint account."

"Where's this going?" I asked.

"For one, where's the rest of the money?" Jared asked rhetorically.

"Don't know," I began, "but I'm sure you're going to tell me."

"Let's get a check going on Linda's bank accounts. That's a lot of money unaccounted for," Jared spoke.

"And, of course, they wouldn't deposit over 10,000 at one time, to avoid having to go into the system. But if we can make sure that freeze stays active on their account, anyone who attempts to deposit into the account, we can assure they're sent to us."

"Let's forget about the money for a second. We've run scans and searches on their accounts for a purchase that could be linked to the prepaid card used for the helicopter, no luck thus far, meaning the card was probably purchased using cash."

"So, we get this call back regarding the ID used to purchase the helicopter, we got our answer to who purchased the helicopter, to say the least."

Jared put the marker down. The board was full of notes containing information pertaining to the case.

"We need to get back on patrol to watch Linda," I spoke.

"You heard Abel's demands," Jared spoke. "You aren't allowed to step foot out of this office for the next few weeks."

"Shit, in a few weeks, Linda will be on her way to Australia," I chuckled. "She's already had a month of a head start since I was in the hospital. Nah, she's not getting away from us."

I stood up from the chair slowly. I limped over to my desk and grabbed my gun. I put it in the holster before grabbing my shield.

"You set?" I asked.

"Let's do it," he spoke as he exited the room.

I walked out of the room behind Jared, turning the light off behind me.

"You want to take the elevator, old man?" he joked as we approached the doors.

"Keep on playin', and I'm gonna elevate my foot up your ass," I chuckled.

Jared pressed the down button on the elevator and we walked inside.

"We taking your car?" Jared asked.

"Nah, let's take your car," I spoke. "Let my baby get some rest."

We exited the elevator and went to the lot. We entered Jared's car.

"Smells good, huh?" Jared chuckled.

"Depends on how you define 'good'," I spoke as I inhaled the new leather smell. Jared had gotten the interior of his car done.

***

"We are sitting outside of Linda's residence. Been out here for about five hours now, but no activity," I spoke over the recorder.

"Why are you recording this?" Jared asked as he fidgeted with his Rubix cube.

"You want me to be suspended?" I joked. "You know I can't radio this shit in. You trying to get me busted, huh?"

Jared laughed.

"Maybe I'll get a chance to shine once that happens," he punched me in the arm.

"You gotta work for it, kid," I spoke with a chuckle as I kept an eye on Linda's home.

"Yeah, whatever."

"You see that?" I asked Jared as I saw Linda's blinds jerk shut.

"Someone's definitely in there," Jared spoke. "Here, climb over to the driver's seat. I'm gonna walk up to the home, and I know you can't run if she tries to jet, so it may be best for you to be able to chase if need be," Jared put his hand on his holster as he exited the vehicle.

"Chicago P.D.!" Jared shouted as he banged on the door.

I watched the home as my phone rang.

"Young, speaking," I answered.

"Richard… interesting news," Madeline spoke. "You know that account you had us watching?"

"Which one?" I chuckled. "Julie's, Michael's, Linda's, or Lisa's?"

"Linda's. There was just a deposit made to the account. Sixty thousand: nine in cash, and 51 via check."

"Well, we know she didn't get that from the department… and she deposited just under the threshold of having to go into the system."

"Wait…" Madeline spoke. "I just refreshed the page. Oh my, God," she spoke.

"What's going on?" I asked.

"There have been six transfers. One was an incoming transfer from a local bank, and the other five were outgoing transfers to external overseas accounts."

"Fuck!" I shouted. "If those external transfers complete, we won't have any way to trace that money. Can you stop it?" I asked her.

"We'll try, but we can't make any promises to it," Madeline spoke. I heard her typing buttons on her computer.

"I gotta go, Madeline. Jared and I will be there momentarily but find out where that check came from. Look at the check image for us."

"Will do," Madeline spoke.

I hung up the phone.

"Yo, Jared," I shouted out the window.

He turned around I motioned for him to come to the car.

He walked over to me.

"What's up?" he asked.

"You know a deposit was just made to Linda's account. 60 thousand."

"Shit," Jared sounded amazed at the amount of money.

"9 in cash, 51 via check. Which would keep her out of the system."

"Well, Linda never was stupid," he remarked. "You think it's her cut?"

"We won't know that until we get that information from the helicopter place. We're wanted back at the station, so let's head back."

Jared walked around to the passenger's side of the vehicle.

"I'll tell you one thing. If that ID comes back as a match to Linda's, all hell is gonna break loose."

"Don't even worry about her," Jared spoke.

"We got to," I replied. "About a minute after the deposit, one large transfer from another bank came through, and five transfers to accounts overseas initiated."

"Like I said, she never was stupid. She knows if that money leaves, it would take forever and eternity to trace it overseas."

"I don't know," I shook my head. "I just want this case to be done with... but you know what; I made a promise. And I can't rest until this case is cracked open."

"You mean 'closed shut'," Jared corrected me.

"That too."

▪▪

"Young, speaking," I answered my office phone.

"Detective Young, how are you? This is Marcus from Heli's Jets calling you back."

"Hey Marcus, how are you? Tell me you got some good news for me."

"Terrific news!" Marcus exclaimed. "Got an ID number for you on that purchase you requested information about. Sorry it took so long to get back to you," he chuckled.

"Four days is quick compared to how long information normally takes," I laughed. "Tell me what you got for me."

"It was an Illinois driver's license that was used to purchase the helicopter."

Marcus read me the ID number and I wrote it down on the notepad.

"You don't happen to have a name with that, do you?" I asked.

"The way our system is set up, it only asks for an ID number. It doesn't have us record the name of the customer. Sorry about that, Detective Young."

"Oh no, it's all good. This information is more than enough. Hopefully, we can crack this case that we're working on."

"I wish you all the best," he added.

"You too," I replied. "Have a good one, Marcus, and thanks again."

"Anytime," he replied. "Bye."

I returned the phone to the receiver and typed the ID number into the system.

I watched as the loading bar appeared on the screen. Surely, this search would take a bit of time, so I locked my office door and walked over to Jared's office.

"What's good?" he asked as I walked into his office. "I see you're walking better. I guess Madison is doing you some justice, huh?" Jared chuckled.

I laughed at his joke.

"The people just called me back. They gave me the ID of the purchaser of the helicopter."

"So, we got a result?"

"I'm not sure, my system is still searching. So, even though that money got away, the bank is insured and will replenish those funds. Plus, we still have that search out so once we find out where it went, we can cut it off."

"Hopefully it gives us insight as to who purchased this helicopter, so we can at least question them on the purchase."

"You and I want the same thing," I spoke to Jared as I pulled out my phone.

"Nope, get off your phone," Jared joked. "You expecting a call from someone?" he teased.

"Shut up," I chuckled. "I'm just looking at the time," I lied.

I hadn't heard from Madison all day and although that wasn't abnormal, I was accustomed to getting random texts throughout the day from her; whether they contained emojis, random jokes, or whatever. I just enjoyed seeing her name appear on my phone.

"You just keep your head on straight," Jared added. "You're useless if you aren't focused, and we need you to finish strong."

"Kiss my ass, man," I chuckled before leaving his office.

I sent Madison a quick text that read 'hey big head' before locking my phone and returning it to my pocket.

I unlocked my computer once I entered my office.

I immediately picked up my phone and called Abel.

"Abel, it's her!"

"What do you mean?" he asked.

"The guy from the helicopter place called," I began, "and gave me the ID of the person who purchased the helicopter. I did a search in the system, and it's Linda's ID." I rose from my chair, put the call on speaker, and began to pace the floor before continuing. "She was the one who purchased the helicopter; she just had major deposits and transfers to and from her account, she's been running from us... it's Linda. She's the inside woman giving them all they need to know."

"Alright, so this is what I want you to do. Get some officers down and take Julie and Michael to separate interrogation rooms. Then, you're to send two more over to get Linda and bring her in for questioning," he spoke. "When you interrogate Julie and Michael, you need to speak as if Linda's already confessed to the crime. Hell, do whatever it takes to get those two on pins and needles."

"Some may call that fishing," I chuckled as I secured my weapon.

"Yea, but I call it getting the job done. There's a reason we're number one in the city, Young. Let's not fuck it up."

Abel disconnected the call and I locked my screen.

I put my badge in my pocket and closed my office door. I walked over to Jared's office and stood in the doorway before tapping on the glass.

"Let's go, sweetheart," I joked. "Abel said to get our black asses over to Linda's and pull her in while she's kicking and screaming."

"He did not say that," Jared chuckled.

I laughed.

"Nah, but he did say that we, not us directly but officers in general, need to get Linda down here for questioning, and to begin questioning Julie and Michael in separate rooms. I looked at my wristwatch. "Truth be told, I wanna do it all."

"Still trying to be top cop, huh?" Jared asked. "I'm not trying to knock your hustle or anything," he rose to his feet, "but you gotta take it easy until you're fully healed," he put his hand on my shoulder.

"What could a little questioning hurt?" I asked.

Jared gave me a stern look.

"Lighten up, Chief. We'll go down and begin to question Julie and Michael, send some officers over for Linda, and we'll question her." I turned and headed for the door but discreetly massaged my thigh; I was beginning to feel pain, but I didn't want Jared to worry.

Jared walked out of his office behind me and locked the door.

We got on the elevator and rode it down to the first floor. While the elevator descended, Jared called for a few officers to drive over and pick up Linda. Surely, she would try to run again if she saw us, but she may have given different officers a little leeway.

Two officers were escorting Julie and Michael to separate interrogation rooms as we exited the elevator.

"So, how do you wanna do this?" Jared asked me. "Who do you wanna take?"

"Lemme take on Julie," I told him.

"Do not let her get in your head," Jared asserted. "You know she's going to try to push your buttons."

"Yeah, I'm not going to let that happen," I spoke before shaking Jared's hand.

Jared walked into the room with Michael and I walked into the adjacent room with Julie.

"Make yourself comfortable," I spoke to her.

"Why was I not surprised when they said that you wanted to speak with me?" she asked as she sat back in the chair.

"You probably know you've done something wrong, or have fucked up in some fashion," I spoke to her.

I walked to the opposing side of the table so I could face her.

"But tell me how much you had to pay Linda to get her to purchase the helicopter for you all to use in the robbery," I spoke to Julie.

"I keep telling you, I don't know what the hell you're talking about. I've never flown a helicopter, so asking me to fly one would be suicide," she remarked.

"I never said you were the pilot," I spoke as I placed the image down on the table in front of her. "You were the robber."

Julie studied the images that the security camera captured.

"Yeah, you did really well. Almost had me and this whole unit fooled; that it, until you slipped up. You thought you'd disabled every camera, but you didn't. There was one right on the roof capturing your entrance, and one posted by the stairs that watches the entire east wing of the branch."

I paced the floor again to exercise my leg.

"Not to mention, Linda's 61-thousand-dollar deposit tells it all." I chuckled aloud. "And not only did she make a large deposit, she received a larger deposit from a local bank, but not before initiating 5 overseas transfers."

Julie studied my face for signs of a lie.

"How's your leg, Detective? I see you're moving quite a bit," Julie chuckled.

"Don't be a smartass, Julie," I shouted in her face.
"The fuck does Linda depositing her money have to do with me?" she snarled.

"The first one to confess gets the deal," I added. "And Linda just took that deal. So, I'm breaking the rules to help you out," I lied to her, but refused to show it.

As I said that Linda confessed, spots of Julie's face turned red.

"You're lying," she spoke as her normal skin tone arrived. "Richard, if Linda confessed to anything, which I have no idea what you're referring to, why are you sitting here talking to me? The case would be closed shut and you'd be resting. Shouldn't you be at home?" she asked. "How's that leg doing? You never answered my question," she laughed.

"Hahaha," I sarcastically laughed. "Everybody's a comedian now," I spoke.

"I'm concerned for your well-being," Julie smirked.

"Why don't we just stick to the topic?" I asked. "So, this is how this is going to work."

I sat down across from her.

"You're going to sign this paper, confessing to the crimes you've committed; you're going to write the code down to stop those transfers from leaving the country, and you're going to submit a public apology to Jennifer Lawrence and the staff of her bank. You do this, you'll be out in 5 years, tops."

Julie looked at me inquisitively.

"Nah, I don't think I want to do that."

"You sure you wanna go away for ten years?"

"I'm not going away, because I didn't do shit," Julie started. "I'll take my day in court."

"You're willing to risk it all?" I asked. "Once I exit this room, this deal goes with me and you'll never see it again."

I placed the images in the folder.

"I'll see you later, Richard," Julie spoke.

I walked over and tapped on the window and an officer walked inside.

"Get this piece of trash out of my sight," I uttered to him.

I glanced at Julie and she had a devious smile on her face.

The officer helped her rise to her feet.

"As I said before: if you had shit on me, we wouldn't be having this discussion," Julie spoke as she was escorted out of the door.

I followed her and the officer out of the room.

Part of me felt accomplished, but the other part was still a little down.

I answered my phone on the first ring.

"Hello?" I spoke.

"Hey, you," Madison spoke.

"Hey," I replied; a smile formed across my face.

"How are you doing today?" she asked in a soft tone.

"I'm pretty well. You caught me as soon as I got out of an interrogation," I chuckled.

"I'm sorry, baby," she spoke. "I just took my first break; it's been busy around here. Should I call you back?" she asked.

"You're good, Madison," I spoke to her. "I'm just glad you didn't call about 5 minutes ago because I wouldn't have been able to answer," I joked.

"You're silly," Madison giggled. "I take it you all are busy there, too," she spoke.

"Well, we got a break in a case we're working on, so we're trying to put the finishing touches on everything. I can tell you about it later."

I saw two officers walk in with Linda. She wasn't resisting or fighting back; she seemed rather calm.

Linda saw me and quickly looked away.

"He's not interrogating me, is he?" she whispered to the officer.

"Luckily for you…" the officer began.

Linda let out a sigh of relief before the officer continued.

"He is."

"Is this the case you were telling me about involving the bank?" Madison asked.

"Yep, that's the one. I'll admit that the ringleader of this fiasco was pretty smart," I joked as I thought of Julie.

"I know you wanna go on and crack this case," Madison began. "Let me let you go," she finished. "We'll speak later, babe."

"Alright, baby," I spoke.

"Bye."

"Bye," I ended the call and returned my phone to my pocket.

Jared exited the interrogation room and dried his hands on a napkin.

"Any luck?" I asked.

"He's not cracking," Jared answered. "How about you with Julie?"

"She's not talking either," I laughed. "It's amusing how coordinated these two are," I mentioned.

"They've thought this shit out," I laughed. "They may be smarter than we thought they were," Jared spoke.

"Yeah, but they can't outsmart us," I added. "Julie and Michael are both simple; they just want to get away with the crime that they committed."

Jared and I walked to the room that Linda was led to.

"And so, they've created a story and explanation to have us running in circles and included Linda in it to fuck with our heads even more." I finished as we opened the door.

"Shit's working, though," he added.

We walked into the room and saw Linda handcuffed to the table.

"So, this is what you've been up to?" Jared asked as he sat down.

I couldn't fix my mouth to say anything to Linda. I was filled with disgust at the stunt she'd pulled.

"I know how this works," Linda spoke. "You all may deny it, but I'm one of you, so I know all of the tricks and schemes. So, what's good?" Linda sat back in the chair.

"The floor is yours," Jared spoke. "I'm assuming you know why you're here."

Linda looked at me.

"Actually, I don't. Because I didn't do shit," she defended.

"Why the fuck did you run from us if you didn't do shit?" I finally spoke.

If Linda wanted to play these mind games, I was going to give her what she wanted.

"If the cops come to your door banging and knocking, it's never a good sign. Especially if you're one of them and haven't been to work. And just in hearing the tone of your voice," Linda spoke, "I did what I had to do. I knew I'd have to face you sooner or later, so here I am," Linda adjusted herself. "Woman to man."

"That's bullshit," I responded. "As we both know, you're a cop yourself, so you know how bad it can get if we have to chase someone. I think you're full of shit," I raised my tone.

"Richard, it's cool," Jared touched my shoulder to remind me to calm down. "Linda, we're not going to play these mind games. Simply put, we know you're working with Julie and Michael. We know you purchased the helicopter for them to use in the robbery."

"Go on," Linda smirked.

"You being a smartass?" I asked her.

Linda grinned at me.

"You're lucky I don't want to lose my job over a piece of shit like you," I told her.

"Richard…" Jared spoke as he got up and walked over to the window sill, where a folder lied.

He picked it up and walked back over to the table.

"I'll be quiet," I quickly replied.

"Let's talk about these deposits and the outgoing transfers," Jared continued as he opened the folder and laid the contents on the desk.

Linda looked at the papers but didn't say a word.

"So, what?" she finally spoke. "I make money, I deposit it and store it in an off-shore account. Is that a crime?"

I decided to take another approach with her. She was right, she was one of us, so our usual interrogation methods wouldn't work on her.

Since I was her partner, I knew her better than anyone else in the unit, so I felt I'd have a good chance at tugging at what I knew to get a confession out of her.

"Linda, how long ago did we begin working together?" I calmly asked.

Linda was silent.

"No, seriously. Tell me when you became my partner."

"Roughly three years ago, I gotta hand it to you, Richard, we were some tough cookies. Not too many people would have entered the unit straight out of school."

"But we did it," I began. "Which is why I don't understand why you would act like this."

Linda's smirk faded. "What is it that I'm doing? Some things came up, and I wasn't able to work. I wasn't about to bring those issues with me."

"If something was going on, you could have come to me, of all people in this unit," I added.

Jared didn't say a word; he knew the angle I was taking with Linda and didn't want to interfere.

"I've been through so much shit in the past few weeks. I was almost killed in an explosion that *your* prints were involved with; I have to take pain pills for my leg because of an accident that occurred about a month ago. It's been one thing after another."

"My prints?" Linda asked, seemingly confused. "Are you accusing me of trying to kill you?"

"To kill someone," I spoke.

I lowered my tone and eased my breathing to calm down.

"I've been your partner for far too long for you to feel that you couldn't come to me about anything. I would have listened to you regardless," I added.

Linda caught on to what I was doing.

"There was nothing to come to you about," her smirk returned. "Because I didn't do shit," she finished.

"You know what," I stood up. "You handle this," I spoke to Jared. "I was trying to give you a way out," I mentioned to Linda. "But you, you're a special kind of stupid."

Jared shook his head.

"Linda, it's back to me," he cleared his throat. "Tell me about this deposit. And don't try to say it's from the department because the department hasn't done any deposits to your account, especially of that great amount. You haven't even been to work," Jared chuckled.

Linda remained quiet.

"I take it that this is the part where you all expect for me to say I want my lawyer, yes?" she asked after moments of silence.

Jared looked at her.

"It's not going to happen," she chuckled.

"We have proof, Linda," I spoke again. "It's over. We know you purchased the helicopter for Julie and Michael to use. We know they're having you store the money in an offshore account to avoid having it trace back, we know you tried to kill an officer. We know it was you!"

It was taking every ounce of loving my job to restrain myself from attacking Linda.

"Richard," she adjusted herself. "Let me save you the trouble. 'Linda Jackson, you have the right to remain silent. Blah, blah, blah,'" she chuckled.

"It's funny to me how you think this is a game," I added. "Let's see how much you're smiling in a cell." I tapped on the glass before pulling out my handcuffs and passed them to Jared.

"It kills me to do this," Jared began. "Linda Jackson, you are under arrest for being an accomplice to the robbery of the Esther Community Bank."

Linda's smirk left immediately.

"You have the right to remain silent. Anything you say can and will be used against you in the court of law."

The realization of what was occurring was finally falling upon Linda, and she looked as though she was about to collapse.

"You have the right to an attorney," Jared continued. "If you cannot afford an attorney, one will be appointed to you. Do you understand these rights in which they have been given to you?" he finished.

Linda didn't answer. She still looked as though she was just hit in the stomach and was out of breath.

"Yeah, she understands," I spoke. "Get her ass out of here."

An officer walked into the room and took Linda by the arm. They both walked out of the room.

As the two walked down the corridor, many officers glared at Linda. They were in disbelief, as I was, that one of their own would do something like this.

Linda kept her head down as she entered the main hallway. She didn't dare lock eyes with anyone, especially not Abel.

12

"So, we've got a positive ID on the helicopter purchase, Linda's prints on the gas line, Julie and Michael were identified at the robbery; we need to go on and close this case," Jared spoke as he dribbled the basketball between his legs.

Although we weren't at work, this case was a major concern for me.

"I wish it was that simple, but it isn't," I spoke to Jared as I stole the ball from him and dribbled it. "You know probable cause doesn't sit well in court," I added.

Jared kept his eye on the ball as it dribbled. As I tried to run in and dunk the ball in the basket, he intentionally fouled me.

"Son of a bitch," I chuckled as I threw the ball away and walked back to the line.

"Nope, that was *not* about to happen today," Jared laughed. "Try again," he spoke as he passed me the ball.

He passed me the ball and I immediately shot a three-pointer. The ball went through the basket: nothing but net.

"My biggest fear at this point is that Linda finds a way or a loophole to get out of prison based on hearsay," I dribbled the ball as Jared passed it to me.

"Yeah; we let her slip, we're not getting her back," Jared added. "Julie and Michael may be smart, but they don't have shit on Linda. The fact that she's one of us will make the shit impossible to get her back. She knows the system."

Jared reached and attempted to steal the ball but slapped my hand instead.

"Fuckin' foul, man," I groaned with a slight chuckle.

"I'm just trying to play," Jared laughed as he passed me the ball.

I pump-faked the shot and Jared jumped to try to block the shot. While he was in the air, I ran to the basket and dunked the ball with one hand.

"That's game!" I exclaimed.

"It's all good," Jared joked as I picked up the ball and walked to the back door.

I sat down on the couch and turned on the television; Jared did the same.

"Tomorrow, we go in with a fresh mind," I spoke. "We have the three right where we want them to be; now, we just have to build a solid case against them."

"You think Abel has stripped Linda of her badge and everything yet?" Jared asked.

"I know he has."

....

"Young, we have a situation," Abel spoke as he entered my office, frantically.

"What's going on?" I asked as I ensured my gun was in the holster.

"It's Linda. She's not in the cell and all of her belongings are gone."

"What the fuck?" I spoke as I followed him out of the office.

"Now, we're all suiting up to go find her," Abel spoke. "Unfortunately, she's still one of us."

"You didn't have her removed from the system?" I asked.

"There's a process that has to be followed under circumstances like this. Plus, none of the officers have been to her home to clear her of her backup badge or weapons."

"So, she could be out there parading around like one of us," I shook my head.

"Let's hope not," Abel spoke.

I stopped at Jared's office.

"Linda's gone," I spoke as I peeked in the door.

"The fuck?!" Jared asked as he stood up. "How?"

"I don't know... well, Abel doesn't know. But this is what happens when you know the system. We gotta go," I spoke.

While Jared was grabbing his gun and coat, a vision came to me and I entered my trance.

Seconds later, I came back into reality and I rushed over to Jared's phone.

"Rick, what's wrong?" he asked.

"It's Linda... she's going to call to get Julie and Michael transferred, but in reality, she's going to be the one to pick them up and take them away from here."

I picked up the phone and called downstairs.

"Isabella," I hurried.

"Hey, Richard," she recognized my voice. "What's going on?"

"Listen, do this favor for me. If a call comes in to transfer Julie and Michael to a different precinct, deny the request."

"Oooh," she sucked air through her teeth. "I think the other operator has already approved the request. They've already been moved out," Isabella spoke. "What's wrong?"

"Shit," I spoke. "That wasn't an authorized transfer. Shut the facilities down and activate their trackers," I spoke before hanging up.

Almost immediately, the alarms started sounding within the building.

"Let's go," I spoke to Jared and we exited his office.
As we walked down the hall, we heard inmates shouting racial slurs at us and calling us idiots because the building was on lockdown.

"How the fuck do you let an inmate escape?"

"That's what happens when an inmate is a cop. They look the other way."

"Fuckin' pigs," an inmate spat out of his cell.

The spit missed Jared and me and we kept walking to get to the front.

"Do we have a location on Linda?" I asked.

"Not yet," Abel spoke as many officers gathered around a computer screen.

"What about the trackers on Julie and Michael?" Jared looked at the screen. "You know that she picked them up."

"We're not getting a hit from either tracker. We gotta face it, Linda's one of us; she knows all the tricks."

"Not all of them," I spoke as I pulled my car keys from my pocket. "Okay, everyone, listen up." I projected. "So, we know Linda... and she's one of us," I ensured I had a loaded magazine in my gun. "It's going to take all of us working together to take her down. She knows nearly every angle that we're going to approach her with, so taking her one on one would be stupid and ineffective." I gave the team a small pep talk.

"If you come in contact with Linda, sole apprehension could be considered suicide," Jared continued. "While she has not shown deadly force or violence, she is trained to do so, so for everyone's safety, let's use extreme caution in apprehending her."

"Let's move out," I spoke as the officers put on their jackets.

Jared and I left the building and walked to my vehicle.

I opened my trunk and grabbed the mirror to check under the vehicle.

"Can't be too careful, you know?" I chuckled while ensuring my vehicle wasn't tampered with.

"Not with Linda running around," Jared spoke. "I don't blame you," he spoke as he observed.

As I finished the inspection, I returned the extended mirror to the trunk and unlocked the doors.

Jared and I both climbed inside before I drove out of the lot.

"How's your leg?" Jared asked me.

"It's cool," I spoke. "As you can tell from that ass-whoopin' I gave you in basketball the other day, I'm much better than I was," I laughed.

"Yeah, yeah," Jared rebutted. "I just want to ensure that my boy is at his peak and is ready to pursue Linda."

"I'm set. Just know that when we apprehend her, she's not going to know what hit her."

I took a look in my rearview mirror before accelerating.

"We're going in hot," I exerted.

Jared ensured his seatbelt was fastened before making a phone call.

"All officers, report to Linda Jackson's residence. We'll develop a step-by-step upon arrival, if she isn't present," I spoke over the radio.

"The GPS signal of the tracker for Michael Wilson has returned," Isabella transmitted.

"Perfect," I replied. "What's the location?"

"It's right around the corner from the station," Isabella sounded confused. "And it's moving."

"What the fuck?" Jared spoke to me.

"Any luck on Julie's tracker?" I asked.

"None," Isabella spoke. "Michael's tracker is approaching the station."

"Keep some officers in the front. If Michael enters that station, we need the ultimate protection for everyone in there. There's no telling why he's returned."

I turned my radio down and continued to speed towards Linda's residence.

Moments passed as we all sped down the expressway towards Linda's.

As we got off the expressway, Isabella sent a transmission through the radio.

"Michael Wilson has entered the police station. Subject is unarmed but is pleading to prove his innocence in the robbery trial."

"10-4," I spoke. "Put the subject in a holding cell until we return to base."

"I wonder what that's all about," I questioned aloud.

"Shit," Jared began, "I hate to admit it, but with Michael returning to the station, it could prove innocence."

"That's gotta be the craziest idea I've ever heard... but I admit, there may be some truth to that. Either way," I merged off the expressway and turned right, "we need to get Linda before we move forward."

Moments later, we were turning down Linda's street.

I knew that the sirens would scare her away if she were at home, but I didn't care.

"Be vigilant for anything suspicious. Remember, she's expecting us," Jared spoke.

I stopped directly in front of Linda's home and closely observed the home; paying meticulous attention to detail.

Through the planks in her fence, I noticed her garage door closing.

"Like that," I spoke to Jared.

I accelerated quickly and turned the corner as I approached the intersection.

"We've got motion around Linda's garage," I alerted over the radio.

I turned down her alley to discover a vehicle exiting from the opposite end.

"We got an unidentified vehicle leaving the alley, going westbound," Jared spoke over the radio.

I turned on my siren lights and sped down the alley when I saw two officers follow directly behind the vehicle.

"We have a positive ID on the suspect traveling in the vehicle," an officer spoke over the radio. "It's Linda Jackson."

"All units, move," Abel spoke as I exited the alley.

I turned behind the vehicle, and Linda began to accelerate once she saw my vehicle in her rearview mirror.

"All units, be advised. We are in pursuit of a blue Pontiac heading southbound on Western. The suspect is a former Chicago police officer."

Linda didn't look over to my vehicle as she sped.

"Pit her in," Jared spoke to me.

"I'm moving in to attempt to pit her," I spoke over the radio as I applied the brakes to slow down.

As the front of my vehicle aligned with the back of Linda's, I tried to make the grill guard hit the rear-side of her vehicle.

Although there was a collision, Linda prevented her car from spinning out and stalling, by performing a 360 as I hit the back of her vehicle.

"Fuck!" I shouted as I looked in my rearview and saw Linda trailing me.

"Pit maneuver failed," Jared spoke over the radio. "We're going to attempt it again," he added as I slowed down.

I looked at Linda and she looked at me before winking.

Linda accelerated and passed my vehicle.

"Clear the way, boys," I spoke as I aligned the front of my vehicle with the back of hers.

I quickly swerved into the back of her vehicle; instead of doing a 360, she performed a 180 and proceeded to drive in the opposite direction.

"Abel, she's coming directly for you," I spoke as I slowed down and quickly turned my steering wheel all the way to the left.

"She's truly one of us," Jared spoke. "She knows all of the tricks we're going to hit her with."

"That' why we improvise," I added as I made a left turn down a side street, followed by a right.

"The surprise attack," Jared began. "But in your personal vehicle?"

"Gotta sacrifice my baby," I spoke. "Hope we're insured."

"You know we haven't been cleared to attempt this," Jared chuckled but I could hear fear and panic in his voice.

"We took an oath to protect these streets by any means necessary. That includes this," I accelerated more.

"Suspect has just caused four officers to collide," Abel spoke over the radio. "Young, report with your location."

"Coming in hot," I spoke. "Is she still northbound on Western?" I asked.

"Yes. Approaching 79th and Western now," Abel answered.

"10-4," I looked at my current location.

"We're about 7 blocks ahead of them... make this right," Jared spoke. "Cut them off at 72nd."

I made the right turn and began to speed down the street. As I approached the intersection, I saw Linda's vehicle beginning to pass by.

"Punch that shit," Jared spoke and he persuaded me to collide with her vehicle.

I switched gears and accelerated.

"This might hurt," I told Jared. "Let's fucking go, Linda," I yelled.

I drove through the intersection at nearly 65 miles-per-hour and rammed the side of Linda's car.

The impact released such force, that Linda's window shattered immediately upon collision.

"Shit," Jared coughed.

Smoke emitted from my engine as both vehicles stalled.

"Fuck!" I spoke as I held my head.

I heard police sirens around me, as well as an ambulance siren approaching.

It was impossible to open either of her doors, considering her car was pushed into a sturdy brick building.

Many officers exited their vehicle and ran towards Linda's car. Although my head was bleeding and my car was ultimately destroyed, I managed to switch my car into reverse and I reversed from the collision to allow access to her door.

Many officers ran in and aimed their weapons. An officer opened the door.

Linda was slumped over the steering wheel. The front and side airbags released upon collision.

"Let me see your hands," Abel shouted.

Linda didn't reply.

Officer McKenzie radioed for an ambulance while Madeline and a few other officers walked over to my vehicle.

"You okay?" Madeline asked me as she attempted to help me out of the vehicle.

I coughed and held my hand over my head.

"Yeah, I'm good," I spoke as I emerged from the vehicle.

"You sure?" She questioned as another officer assisted Jared.

"I'm good. J, you cool?" I shouted.

"Besides the fact that you just almost killed us," he chuckled, "I'm all good."

I'd put Jared and my life in danger... over Linda; the realization was just settling in.

Loyalty; that's the code I'd lived by, and when I'd signed up to be an officer, loyalty is what kept me in line, and for Linda to turn her back on the force, pushed me to a place that I didn't want to be.

An ambulance approached the scene as more officers arrived and blocked the street to prevent traffic from passing by.

"She's not responsive," Officer McKenzie shouted.

"Wake her ass up," I replied to him. "She's not hurt."

I held my shoulder. After the collision, I was in pain in multiple areas of my body.

Officer McKenzie put his fingers on her neck.

"There is a pulse," he spoke as the paramedics wheeled the stretcher over.

They managed to pull Linda from the vehicle and onto the stretcher.

"Is Julie in there?" Jared called out.

"She's here," another officer called as they pulled her from the vehicle with her hands raised.

"They're going to run them both over to the hospital to check on them and any potential injuries, and once they've been cleared, they'll be transported to the station," I overheard an officer state as Linda was loaded into an ambulance.

"I'm good," Julie spoke. "I don't need to go to the hospital."

"We have to get you checked out," the paramedic told her as he walked her to the back of the ambulance.

"Let's get a few officers to travel to the hospital. I don't want for these two to slip away from us again," Abel spoke.

I lost my balance and stumbled but grabbed onto the door.

"You good, Rich?" Jared asked.

I didn't reply as I was trying to regain my composure.

Two more ambulances arrived on the scene as the two carrying Linda and Julie departed.

A paramedic walked over to me and one walked to Jared and they sat us down on the stretcher.

"Yo, Rich," Jared called out as the paramedic examined him.

"What's up?" I asked.

Jared chuckled before replying.

"You know that was the craziest shit you've done so far, right?"

I looked at my vehicle, the shattered glass and metal debris, and laughed.

"My poor baby," I spoke as the paramedic removed my hand from my head and put a gauze over it.

"Think the department will cover it?" I asked Jared with a laugh.

"Nah, that shit is over with," he laughed in response. "But you did that shit," Jared added. "We got them."

"Yeah, we did," I answered.

From the collision, I had a migraine, but the feeling of joy that I was experiencing overpowered the pain.

"Felony evading to say the least," I spoke in the interrogation room to Linda.

"If you didn't do anything, why'd you flee?" Jared asked.

Linda didn't reply.

"And you're lucky," I added. "You didn't have a scratch on you from the collision.

Linda kept her head down and spoke.

"I want my lawyer," she uttered.

"Oh no, baby girl," I spoke. "The time for lawyers is up." I stood up straight. "Yea, you threw that out the window when you decided to bust out of here and act like you were still an officer."

Linda looked at me devilishly.

"You seem to forget," she spoke, "I'm one of you. I'm entitled to a lawyer, no matter what, and if I decide to lawyer up, you're supposed to take your ass out of this interview room, associate with the fuckers standing behind that window," she pointed to the window, "and get my damn lawyer down here."

I looked at Jared and chuckled.

"That shit is funny," I told Linda. "But you know what? You're right. You *are* one of us," I paced the floor as Jared stood against the wall. "So, you should know, when you're part of this unit, we play by a different set of rules."

"Yeah, like slamming your car into mine to stop me," she retorted. "That shit wasn't legal," she replied.

"What was done, was done for a just reason. Shit wasn't done for fun," Jared replied to Linda. "You know that almost anything goes during a chase, so I don't even know why you ran," Jared remained calm.

"Just go get my lawyer," she rolled her eyes. "I don't have shit else to say to you all."

I slammed my hands on the table and walked out of the room.

"Y'all heard that?" I told the officers as Jared exited the room. "She lawyered up," I chuckled. "I told y'all she would do that shit."

"She's a cop... well, she was a cop. She knows every angle that's coming, so why doesn't she just represent herself?" Officer McKenzie asked.

"Please," I began as I looked through the window at Linda; she had her head down on the desk. "She knows I'd have her ass running in circles if she did that," I cracked my knuckles.

"The lawyer we have on file is 'Lisa Watkins'."

"I figured as much," I chuckled. "Get her ass over here. Tell her that her client needs her."

The officers left the room and Jared stood next to me.

"What's your reply when Lisa gets in?" he asked.

"I truly don't have shit to say to her," I answered. "Our speculations were right though, you see?"

Jared scratched his chin as he looked back through the window at Linda.

"I just can't believe she's acting this way," he spoke.

I looked back at Linda; her head was still down.

"Eh," I started. "I've learned to expect anything from anyone."

I turned back around.

"That way, you lower your disappointment levels when they do something like this."

I closed my eyes as I leaned against the glass.

"This has got you worn out, huh?" Jared asked as he filled a cup with water.

"You got that right," I answered.

Jared took a sip of the water.

"So, now we just wait for Lisa to arrive to continue talking to Linda?"

"Well, we got her on two charges now... well, two charges and one speculation," I chuckled. "File all of them down." I stood up straight. "Oh, and we still have to question Michael on his arrival... see what he's talking about."

"Sounds like he's trying to find a way out."

"Shit, he may be. But, I'm a fair detective. I'll hear you out, and if you convince me, I'll even help you prove your innocence."

Jared and I left the room and walked down the corridor.

"I still can't help but think about my car," I chuckled. "I sacrificed my baby for Linda."

"Knowing all that you do, Roberts is going to try to find a way to help you out. Even though it wasn't an authorized action."

"We got her, right?" I asked.

Jared slightly shrugged his shoulders.

"Well, look who's still walking on two legs after another accident," Isabella spoke and chuckled as we walked past her.

I didn't sustain any broken bones from the collision, just a bruised shoulder, bruised calf, and a cut on my head.

I was beginning to believe that Jared was superhuman. The only injury he'd sustained through the ordeal was a small cut on his arm.

"You got jokes, I see," I joked with Isabella. "Someone's gotta keep this city safe."

"All the officers in this unit, and you feel the need to be superman," she joked as she moved her stray hair away from her face.

"I been trying to tell this man to take it easy," Jared joked. "He's had how many injuries in the past year?" he laughed.

"Yeah, yeah, yeah," I uttered.

"Nah, but for real. Isabella, I know you're the eyes and ears of this unit. Did you hear anything about disciplinary action regarding how Linda was apprehended?"

"No, I haven't heard anything like that," Isabella replied. "Truth be told, I don't see why they would pursue anything. It was a good call," she explained. "But if I do hear anything, I'll be sure to let you all know."

"Thanks," I spoke. "Let us head back here and get Michael. Figure out what's going on with him," I spoke as Jared followed behind me.

"Stay safe out there," Isabella called out.

"I'm anxious to see what Michael has to say," I spoke to Jared. "I mean, come on, there has to be a reason Linda let him go and reactivated his tracker," Jared spoke as we approached the holding cell.

"We'll see."

Jared pulled out his keys and unlocked the cell.

"Michael Wilson," I called.

"That's me," a suspect shouted.

"Now, you know that's me," another guy shouted.

I ignored them and walked towards Michael, although I wanted to tell the others to shut up.

Michael raised his head.

"Come with us," I spoke as I turned around.

Michael followed me out of the cell and Jared closed the door shut.

We escorted him to the closest interrogation room and he took a seat.

Jared closed the door behind himself and I sat directly across from Michael.

"Start talking," I spoke as Jared pulled up a seat alongside me.

"The reason I came back," he began, "is because I'm truly innocent in this whole robbery case."

I looked at him inquisitively.

"If I had a dollar for everyone who's ever told me that, I'd be a millionaire," I chuckled.

"I'm serious right now," he immediately rebutted.

"Michael, do you think we're here to play games right now?"

"At the time of the robbery, I was leaving the doctor's office. I'd been running errands all morning."

"Michael, your DNA was found on top of the bank," I spoke. "Security cameras identify a male as flying the helicopter and witnesses state a male was driving the getaway car." I laid the photos out in front of him.

"Better watch what you say," Jared spoke. "You sure you don't want to lawyer up?

"Lawyer up?" Michael asked. "For what? I didn't do it," he pleaded.

"Okay, Michael. Let's say I entertain your theory that you didn't do it. Explain your DNA being on top of the bank and security cameras placing you there."

Michael paused and examined the images.

"Tick, tick, tick, tick," Jared spoke.

"Truth is, I knew Julie obtained a helicopter. Hell, I was actually kind of excited so I got in the pilot's seat."

"So, you're telling me that Julie was willing to make you an accomplice to a crime?" I looked at Jared, and back to Michael. "It seems like you all were tighter than that."

"I thought so as well," Michael shook his head.

"I guess everything isn't always what it seems," Jared added.

"Long story short, there's a chance that some of my hair was left in the helicopter from when I got inside. I'd just gotten a haircut," Michael added.

"Typical response," Jared uttered.

"My hands are tied," I told Michael. "You gotta try harder to convince me of that. More importantly, I have to present what you're telling me to the DA."

"Go over to St. Mercy's Hospital and speak with Dr. Rutledge. He will testify that I was at his office for a routine checkup at the time of the robbery," Michael immediately refuted. "Check the security cameras."

I looked at Jared and back at Michael.

"If your alibi checks out," I began, "we may have more to talk about. We'll get that information ASAP," I assured Michael.

Even though he'd given us a hard time, previously, I wasn't about making someone pay for a crime they didn't commit. I didn't look at people as being 'guilty until proven innocent', as many officers did.

I rose to my feet and helped Michael to his feet.

We escorted him back to the holding cell and returned to my office.

"I swear that Michael's alibi better check out," I spoke.

"Feels like a wild goose chase," Jared admitted as I logged onto my computer.

"At least it feels like we're making some sort of achievement," I admitted. "Could be closing in on the case."

"It's getting thick though," Jared spoke. "Linda's lawyered up now, and we never expected this from her," he added.

"Expect the unexpected," I replied and my phone rang.

"Young speaking," I answered on speaker.

"Young, Lisa Watkins is here for Linda," Isabella spoke.

"We'll be right down," I told her before hanging up.

"That was pretty fast," Jared told me.

"You're damn skippy," I joked. "Lisa doesn't play any games. But," I began, "we need to be sure to get some officers over to Dr. Rutledge's office and pull those logs and security camera footage."

Before leaving my office, we called Abel and explained the information that Michael told us. He was able to dispatch two available police officers to go to the hospital and obtain the information after they got the warrant approved by the judge.

"Lisa, so good to see you again," I remarked sarcastically as Jared and I entered the interview room.

"Now, why do I get the impression that you're being sarcastic with me, Detective?"

"Only you can tell me why *you* may get a certain impression."

"You just love my clients, huh?" she chuckled.

"It's not even that deep," I answered. "Might we remind you that your client is a former CPD?"

"You do the crime, you do the time," Jared added.

"You know, there are honestly certain circumstances why I even question that people can lawyer up."

"The Chicago Police Department has been after all of my clients for a few months now; I can't even begin to tell you how many times I've seen you all," Lisa chuckled.

"Linda was recently involved in a high-speed pursuit. We're not even talking about the robbery right now," Jared spoke. "We're going strictly off of what we experienced."

"My client was confused at what was going on," Lisa argued.

Jared laughed.

"That's your defense?" I asked. "A former police officer, who's complete medical record is in the system, was going crazy? That'll sit," I entertained her idea.

"What is your beef?" Lisa asked as she sat up.

"Me? I don't have a beef, nor do I hold grudges against anyone. But I have a low tolerance for games and betrayal. It doesn't sit well with me," I replied.

Lisa didn't have an argument to defend Linda fleeing from the police.

"What are you offering?" Lisa surrendered.

"Now she wants a deal," I chuckled at Jared.

"She must be stumped," Jared looked at Linda.

"No deals," Linda spoke.

"What?" Lisa asked as she looked at Linda inquisitively.

"I don't pay you to make deals," she argued.

"Linda," Lisa began.

"Linda, shit," Linda spoke. "I need your help and need to know that you're going to defend me."

"Detectives, can I get a moment to consult with my client?" Lisa asked.

I looked at Jared.

"Sure, take your time," I replied as we left the room.

"You have to realize what you can be charged with if you're found guilty," Lisa whispered as she tried to explain.

"I pay you good money to defend me. Hell, Julie, Michael, and I do. Now if you can't get me off, you need to let me know now."

"You should have thought about this *before* you decided to try to run from your former unit. As an officer, you should know that never works."

"She should just take Lisa's advice," Jared spoke.

"Linda's pride is too large," I shook my head as I watched the two through the window.

Linda didn't have a response to Lisa.

"Now, Linda, I am trying. I came in here trying, but I didn't think you would try to pull this," Lisa spoke in a quiet tone.

"When I pay for a lawyer, I expect them to do whatever it takes to help me. My life is on the line right now," Linda spoke.

Linda knew that the rooms were all armed with microphones, so she made sure to not express anything incriminating.

"I fled because I was scared, and the way I was apprehended, I wish I hadn't been caught," Linda answered. "I was confused as to why my entire unit was chasing behind me and I feared for my life."

"What do you mean the way you were apprehended?" Lisa was confused.

"Richard slammed into the side of my car with his vehicle. *Every* officer in my unit can attest to this," Linda slightly raised her tone.

"That surely can't be safe or legal," Lisa replied.

"It's not safe at all, but as long as he's obtained authorization from his higher, he could do it," Linda spoke. "But I don't even think he obtained authorization. He just did it."

"So, you want to use that as your defense?" Lisa asked.

"What I want is for you to help me, and if you can't do that for certain, you have to let me know."

"There are numerous pending charges against you, Linda," Lisa explained. "And now you add felony evading to the list? How many charges is that now? 2 counts of felony evading, arson and demolition, accomplice to a robbery, *and* money laundering?"

Linda shook her head.

"It's gonna be a tough case," Lisa admitted. "You've run not once, but twice from the police?"

Jared and I knocked on the door and entered the room.

"Bad news for you, Linda, we may be upping your accomplice charge to an active participant charge," I spoke as we brought in a folder.

"What are you talking about?" Lisa asked.

"Your client, Michael Wilson, his alibi checks out. No way was he involved with the robbery of the Ester Communion Bank," Jared spoke.

"He had a doctor's appointment and didn't leave until 2 hours after the robbery concluded."

"Fuck," Lisa whispered.

"Linda, I think you may want to take that deal," I spoke.

Linda didn't say anything.

"What are you offering?" Lisa questioned once again.

"Linda confesses to the crimes, and we minimize her jail time. We'll stick her with the robbery charge, one count of felony evading, and we'll make the demolition and arson charge vanish. She'll do about 7 to 10 years in prison, but the robbery charge will permanently be on her record." I spoke.

"No, I don't like it," Linda spoke.

"Linda, take the deal," Lisa pleaded.

"No, because these charges are ridiculous. I'm not taking the fall for it," Linda argued.

"Linda..." Lisa spoke.

"Lisa, you're fired," Linda spoke. "I need someone that I know can defend me. Not someone who will just give up."

Lisa shook her head.

"Are you sure this is what you want?" she asked.

"Don't let the door hit you on the way out."

Lisa rose to her feet.

"I'm sorry, Lisa," Jared spoke. "We'll escort you to the lobby."

I rose to my feet and the three of us left out of the room; Linda sat in silence.

"I tried," Lisa spoke as we entered the lobby.

"Yeah, but you can't help someone who doesn't want to be helped," I told her.

"The good news is that Michael will be cut loose," Jared spoke optimistically.

"Ah, so now you all realize that he didn't do it," Lisa chuckled.

"Let's not move so fast," I laughed. "Just Michael's alibi is checking out. We still have to go over everything. Everything says that Julie is guilty, for sure."

"You may want to discuss taking a deal with Julie as well," Jared spoke.

"All I can do is defend my clients, that's it," Lisa assured us.

"Even when you know they're guilty..." I uttered.

"Detective, no disrespect intended, but just like you, I have a job to do," she spoke. "And sometimes, it isn't always a pretty result."

"Yeah, well, we shall see the outcome," I spoke to her. "We gotta get back, Lisa, but we'll see you when you meet with Julie again." I shook her hand and walked back to the interview room.

Jared shook her hand and followed.

Linda didn't look up as we entered the room.

"Do you have another lawyer or would you like one appointed to you?" I asked her. "Because, I mean, technically we can't speak to you about confessing, taking a deal, or anything because you've lawyered up."

Linda didn't say a word and kept her head down.

"Linda, we need your answer," Jared spoke.

"Just take me back to my cell," Linda spoke in a low tone.

"Would you like for us to appoint you a lawyer?" I asked again.

"I don't care what you do," Linda sounded as though she gave up. "Just take me back."

Linda rose to her feet and Jared escorted her out of the room.

As Jared walked Linda to her cell, I walked in the opposite direction to get to Abel's office.

"Knock knock," I spoke as a peeked my head through the door.

"Young, what's going on?" Abel asked as he looked up from his paperwork.

"I got a little bit of interesting news for you," I spoke.

"Oh damn," he spoke. "Okay, hit me with it," he closed the open folder.

"We have to take another look at the evidence of this robbery," I explained as I walked into the room and sat down. "Reason is, we may have to cut Michael free."

"And why is that?" Abel asked.

"His alibi checks out," I added. "Dr. Rutledge has Michael Wilson in his office at the time of the robbery up until two hours after. Hospital logs as well as security cameras confirm this."

"Shit," Abel spoke as he pounded his hand on the desk.

"Well, that's why I'm saying we will have to review everything."

"If that's the case," Abel began as he logged into his computer, "we have to determine who was Julie's accomplice was. No way she flew the helicopter, robbed the bank, and drove the getaway car," Abel chuckled. "You thinking Linda did it?"

"As far as I know, Linda can't fly. I have a feeling that if we threw her in a helicopter right now, she wouldn't even know how to start it."

"Do you have *any* leads?" he asked.

"That's why I'm saying we're going to have to go back through the notes," I assured once again.

"You know, we're putting all of our focus on three people," Jared spoke as he walked through the doorway. "But what about considering it to be an inside job?" Jared sat beside me.

"An inside job?" Abel asked.

"Yeah. I mean, okay, let's entertain the idea that Linda may have been the getaway driver, but who was the pilot? We need to check with the bank's employees and look at their 411. Who can fly, who may have ties with Julie Wilson, who may have had a bad experience thus far, and wanted revenge, and more importantly, who called off that day; stuff like that."

Abel had an inquisitive look on his face and spoke moments later.

"I guess you two need to get your asses back out there and do some more detective work."

"Yes, sir," I spoke as Jared and I rose to our feet.

"Quick question," Abel added. "What happened when Linda lawyered up?"

"She fired Lisa," I spoke with a chuckle.

"What? Why?" Abel was dumbfounded. "Lisa was one of the best lawyers, to be honest. You know we hate to hear when someone has lawyered up and Lisa is their lawyer."

"Yea, I know," I joked. "Linda fleeing from us really messed her up. It even had Lisa baffled. We tried to offer a deal but Linda didn't want to take it, so she fired Lisa because she couldn't get Linda off the hook."

"Pathetic," Abel uttered. "Oh well, that's Linda's problem, not ours. You all get out of here."

Jared and I left Abel's office and headed back to the bank.

13

Jared exited my vehicle and I followed behind him into the police station.

"Any luck?" Abel asked as we walked into his office.

"We got a list of all the employees who called off that day."

"About how many employees were out?"

"Roughly 10," I answered.

"Which is a pretty large number for this case. "Have you all begun to narrow it down?"

"Well, only three of them have knowledge of how to fly, but nothing unusual has been occurring on any of their bank accounts," Jared spoke as he scrolled through his phone.

"Okay, cool," Abel rose to his feet and walked to the door.

Jared and I followed him out of the office.

"Do not alert these individuals that they are suspects. We don't need anyone trying to flee before we put a break in the case." Abel walked into the kitchen and poured himself a cup of coffee.

He immediately sipped the coffee after pouring it.

"Oh, so you're just gonna drink it without putting anything into it?" Jared chuckled. "Sugar, cream?"

"I'll add that later. Right now, *you* have to get to work on these clients," he chuckled. "Worrying about my damn coffee."

Jared laughed as he and I left Abel in the kitchen.

"I guess we gotta get to calling these employees," I spoke as we walked to my office.

"Split it 50/50?" Jared asked as he stood in the doorway.

"How about 10/90, you being the 90." I joked. "It's time for you to do some work around here."

"Me? Work?" Jared chuckled. "You should tell yourself that instead of getting injured every few weeks," he laughed.

I was glad that I was cool with Jared before the job even came along. It gave us an advantage when it came time to work together. We could crack jokes at each other and know that they were just jokes; at the end of the day, we could still grab a drink and catch the game at either my home or his home.

Jared stroked his chin hair and laughed.

"Nah, bro, tell you what," he started. "Let's make this easier on both of us. I'll give these employees a call and you can get started on piecing this case back together; substituting Michael for Linda and a potential employee."

"Damn, you're right. We were considering Michael as having flown the helicopter and driving the getaway vehicle."

"Right," Jared added. "Now, I'm not saying that the pilot and driver couldn't be the same person, but either way it goes, it *still* had to be an inside job. Julie was in and out within five minutes and wiped out north of 2 million."

"Unless she and whomever she worked with, have been casing the bank for months. Which isn't impossible. To be honest, it didn't have to be months. The bank's security setup is extremely flawed. No way should a robber have been able to walk away with that kind of money."

Jared made a gun with his thumb, index, and middle finger and pretended to shoot.

"That's the smoking gun," he spoke. "Let's get to it," he walked out of my office and I pulled up the evidence on my computer, as well as the physical evidence.

Three hours passed and I'd compiled a new case; very similar but new. I rose from my seat and walked to Jared's office to present my findings to him.

"I did it!" I spoke, somewhat excitedly.

"You found out the way to meet your bride?" he laughed at his joke.

"Bye, Jared," I flipped him off and walked out of his office.

I turned around and entered his office once again.

"Take two," I spoke. "I got it!"

Jared soulfully laughed.

"Show me what you've got," he spoke after he finished laughing.

"Move this shit," I joked with him as I moved his papers to the side.

"Well, damn," he responded. "This better be good," he chuckled.

"Okay, for real. You know how we've directed all this attention to Michael?"

"Yeah, I know. We gotta switch it up since his alibi checks out."

"Let's swap out Michael for Linda. The flying, the driving, the entire layout could have been garnished by her."

"Keep going," Jared was interested in my theory.

"Being a cop, all Linda has to do is show her badge and fake papers to gain access to the bank. She could have gotten pictures of the security cameras, the bank's structure, policies, and all that."

"That shit is legit, but it's all speculation right now," Jared spoke.

"Speculation unless we can manage to get a confession out of her."

"Good luck with that," he chuckled. "She wouldn't even take Lisa's advice and take the deal."

"Yeah, but we're cops," I reminded him.

"Exactly, so she's going to know our tactics."

"Not all of them," I uttered. "Linda's smart, but she's not as smart as me or you."

"We'll find a way to trap her," he spoke. "What else do you have?"

"No security cameras to capture anything inside of the bank, except for the camera on the roof. So, nothing there. Did they ever pull the surveillance cameras from outside of the bank?" I asked Jared.

"I don't even recall," he admitted. "Probably have to either look through our records or give those stores a call. Perhaps, they have a better glimpse of the face of the getaway driver."

"Precisely... and you know Michael and Linda have very different facial features; eye color, facial structure, all are different."

"But what about the evidence we do have?" Jared asked again.

"It still makes sense if we place Linda is Michael's place. Even at the time of the robbery; I didn't get in contact with Linda until hours after. Who's to say she didn't go home and get settled in?"

"Can't go off of speculation, but it seems solid to me. None of these employees seem to know how to fly or have any grudges against the bank or their managers."

"I'll present this to Roberts and see what he has to say about it. If I get the okay from him, we throw this charge on Linda. If she's backed into a corner, maybe she'll confess," I added.

"Lemme head over there with you. I'm not making any moves with these damn employees," Jared chuckled. "They're seemingly useless right now."

I waited for Jared to lock his system and he followed me to Abel's office.

"You two better have something good for me," Abel spoke as he saw us in his doorway.

"Yeah, I got you some cream and sugar for that dark ass coffee," Jared laughed as he tossed some sugar and cream packets onto Abel's desk.

"Some of us have way too much time on our hands," he shook his head with a slight chuckle.

"Abel, with your permission, we'd like to charge Linda as an active participant in the robbery of the Esther Communion Bank."

"You all pieced everything together?" he asked.

Jared and I sat down and I explained everything to Abel.

"If we replace Michael with Linda, it still makes sense," I explained afterward. "All we're waiting on is footage from the surrounding stores that may have caught something."

"Speaking of which," Abel spoke again, "was the getaway van ever recovered?"

"Damn good question," I answered as I looked at Jared. "I don't think we ever looked in that direction," I shook my head as I felt like a rookie.

Abel laughed.

"Let's find that van. We spent so much time looking for the helicopter that we forgot that the van may hold a clue that we need to lock this case away."

Abel opened a drawer and pulled out his radio.

"Do you all have the license plate of the van?" he asked Jared and me.

I looked through the images and passed him the image that showed the license plate of the vehicle.

"Units on the 'Ester Communion Bank' case, we are on the search for a black Chevrolet Suburban; no city sticker and no tags; license plate Victor-Zebra-3-4-0-James-Igloo."

"10-4," an officer answered over the radio. "We'll be on the lookout."

"Wanna head over towards Linda's place?" I asked Jared. "We find this van and it places Linda at the scene, we can only use that as additional evidence when throwing this charge on her."

"Yeah, I'm down," he spoke.

"Let's do the damn thing," I spoke as we left to his vehicle.

"As much as we're out of the office in our personal vehicles, they're going to think we're playing games," Jared jokingly suggested.

"Eh, they'll be alright," I spoke as I looked at the police station while climbing inside of his vehicle.

"You think Linda's gonna take a deal?" Jared asked.

"I don't know, but I'll tell you this much. If we locate that van and can place her inside of the vehicle, she'll be crazy if she doesn't," I answered as I turned up the radio.

The drive consisted of music and jokes passed back and forth between Jared and me, and minutes later, he was driving in front of Linda's home.

We both exited the vehicle and walked inside of Linda's gate into her backyard.

We walked directly to her garage and looked through the window.

"Nothing's here," I spoke the obvious.

"Linda isn't crazy. She knows that putting that van here is damn near turning herself in," Jared replied. "Nah, we gotta find something that can give us a clue."

"Thanks, Captain Obvious," I replied.

"You're the one to talk, huh?" he referred to my earlier comment.

I laughed at his comment.

"You're damn right, I am. Maybe an extra set of keys or a carved off-key for a van."

"Or we could let the others find the van and we do the searching," Jared joked.

"We could, but that's not how we do shit," I replied.

We walked back to Jared's vehicle and climbed inside. "This is Officer Riker, badge number 2909. We've located an abandoned 4-door suburban. Same license plate as called in earlier." An officer spoke over the radio in a gruff tone.

"See," Jared replied. "Sometimes, you just let that shit ride and it will come to you," he gave me the side-eye before picking up the radio. "This is Officer Hubbard. Radio in with your location; we're on our way over there."

Jared started the vehicle and drove away from Linda's home.

"Vehicle is on the corner of 119th and Halsted," Officer Riker spoke.

"What the fuck?" I spoke aloud to Jared. "That's on the south side."

"Yeah, they made sure we wouldn't trace the shit back," he sped off.

"Tape off the area," I spoke over the radio. "Make sure no one touches that van."

"10-4," Officer Riker replied.

"Let's hurry and get there," I spoke to Jared. "I'm about ready to shut this case closed," I closed my eyes.

"The crazy thing is," Jared began to weave in and out of traffic, "as soon as we seem to make progress, something else comes up. It's like this shit is never going to end."

"Oh, it will," I spoke. "All good stories have an ending."

My cellphone rang and I looked at the caller ID.

"Hey baby," I answered.

"Hey babe," Madison replied. "I decided to run out to grab a bite with my coworkers so I thought I'd give you a call and see how you're doing."

Jared made mimicking faces at me, as to resemble what I looked like while talking to Madison.

I flipped him off with a silent chuckle and proceeded to talk.

"Oh, word?" I asked. "That's what's up, babe. I'm just sitting in the car with Jared; we're on our way to test this van that was just identified as the getaway vehicle. But you know I can't discuss the case too much," I laughed. "You trying to get me fired, babe?"

"Not even," she chuckled. "It's always something exciting going on on your end."

"I wish," I laughed. "Not too much action right now."

"Sounds more thrilling than what I'm going through," Madison chuckled. "But babe, I'm gonna let you go. I just wanted to hear your voice. I'll see you tonight," she blew a kiss on the phone.

"You most definitely will," I replied. "I'll see you later, baby," I spoke.

"Okay, babe." She hung up.

"Man, that chick has you sprung," Jared chuckled.

"Just drive the damn car," I playfully responded.

■ ■

"What happened with that van?" Abel asked as we reentered the police station.

"We got her," I mouthed to him.

Abel patted me on the back as we passed him.

Jared walked towards Linda's cell and I followed.

"Linda Jackson," I shouted as he unlocked the door.

Linda slowly approached us.

I walked her out of the cell and over to the interrogation room. Jared trailed behind us as an escort to the room.

"What is it this time?" she asked.

"Linda, we're adding the robbery to your list of charges," I spoke.

After all that Linda and I had been through, I figured it would be hard to arrest her and prosecute her; I was wrong.

"No way," she replied in a surprised tone.

"Security cameras outside of the bank have captured you driving the getaway vehicle to leave." Jared reluctantly spoke. He seemed more affected by this than I was.

"Now, you did lawyer up," I spoke. "So, we will honor your wish before we continue. Is that how you wish to proceed?"

Linda was silent. She didn't know of any lawyers who'd be able to pull strings to get her off; she knew that Lisa was her best option in this scenario.

"Call Lisa," Linda spoke.

***

Lisa entered the room and shook hands with Jared and me.

"Hello, Detectives," she spoke as she sat down.

"Good to see you again, Lisa," I answered.

"Do you need a moment with your client?" Jared asked her.

"Brief me on the charges as well as the offer again."

"Without taking a deal," I spoke, "Linda's looking at 2 counts of felony evading, arson & demolition, one count of robbery, and money laundering."

"And what are you proposing?" Lisa asked.

Linda was silent and allowed Lisa to do the talking.

"Here's what we can do: Linda pleads guilty, and we will drop one of the evading charges, and the arson and demolition charges will vanish. She lets us know the information to the external accounts that the money has been dispersed into, and we can also eliminate the money laundering charge. But, the robbery charge will stick," Jared spoke.

"She serves seven-to-ten years in prison, and within five years of being released, she can have the charges dropped from her record; every charge except the robbery charge," I lightly tapped my foot on the floor.

Lisa looked at Linda, and Linda looked back at Lisa.

Jared and I showed no emotion as the two observed each other.

"It's a pretty good deal, Linda," Lisa spoke.

"And what happens if I don't take the deal?" Linda asked.

"Well, Linda, you're a cop," I responded almost immediately. "You should know the repercussions of your actions."

I was growing impatient with Linda being difficult.

"With all of the charges we have against you, Linda, you don't take the deal," Jared began, "you're looking at a minimum of 25 years."

Linda thought for a moment and nudged Lisa lightly.

"Can I get one more moment to discuss with my client?" Lisa asked.

"Take your time," Jared spoke. "Come on, B," he rose to his feet.

I followed him out of the room.

"She may be getting ready to crack," Jared answered. "Linda doesn't want to do 25 years."

"Hell," I replied. "She doesn't want to do one year. Linda's scared shitless right now," I assured Jared as we looked through the glass.

"What do you think?" Lisa asked Linda.

"Put up some kind of fight," Linda pleaded. "Negotiate with them. That 25 years will not do me justice, and as you said, if we take this to trial, it will be a hard case."

"I'll do what I can," Lisa answered. "But you have to trust me on this. This deal will be best for you in the long run."

Linda sighed.

"Okay," she surrendered.

"Should we go back in?" Jared asked.

"Nah, give them about ten minutes. Meanwhile, bae calls," I chuckled as I pulled out my phone and walked towards the kitchen.

"Sprung ass," Jared shouted with a laugh.

"Don't be mad because your bae doesn't love you," I joked.
***
Minutes passed before I returned to the interrogation room.

"Everything okay?" I asked as I returned into the room with Jared.

"Detectives, I would like to negotiate with you regarding this offer," Lisa spoke.

"I'm listening," I almost immediately replied.

"Linda releases the information to the accounts that the money was dispersed to, and you all cut the sentence down to five-to-seven years in prison, with the possibility of parole in three. I'm sure since this is my client's first offense, and that my client is one of your own, the DA will consider a little leniency," Lisa spoke.

I looked at Jared, but I had to remember that the priority was to be able to put a criminal away for this crime.

Jared looked at me and nodded. We both knew Abel would approve of this motion.

"Linda confesses to the crime and releases the information to the accounts so that we can retrieve the money and return it, she'll serve five-to-seven years in prison. We can't promise the possibility of parole." I spoke.

Linda nodded her head to Lisa.

"You got a deal," Lisa spoke.

"I'll go get the paperwork drawn up," Jared spoke as he left out of the room.

Lisa whispered to Linda.

The only thing that I could think about was catching Julie or getting her to confess to the crime.

I grabbed the pen and pad from the window sill.

"Here," I spoke to Linda, "you know how this goes," I told her. "I want you to verbally tell me what happened, as well as give me a written confession. I also need for you to write down those account numbers."

Linda looked at me.

"This confession is for me. I'm only giving *my* side of the story."

"Fair enough," I replied.

"I was approached about a job," she began. "I was told there's a ton of money to be made off of it. I was told that I would have to do a little flying and driving, that's it. So, I went by the bank and scoped out the place. Layout and all. I flew the helicopter above the bank, and my partner rappelled from the helicopter through the glass roof of the bank."

"Your partner?" I questioned as I reached for a name.

"I told you, this confession is only for me."

"You're right," I spoke. "Go on."

"Once my partner was inside the bank, I flew the helicopter to a vacant field and destroyed it. I got inside of the van and drove back to the bank. I drove through the south entrance and exited through the north, and once we were clear, we abandoned the vehicle and I returned home, where I prepared to continue as a police officer."

I was disgusted at Linda but I didn't say anything.

She wrote down her confession and I excused myself from the room.

I found myself walking to Abel's office, and as I was walking, I had a vision come to my mind. I came back to reality almost immediately and proceeded.

"Abel, we gotta cut Michael loose," I spoke. "Linda's just confessed, but there is a catch."

Abel looked surprised.

"I'm surprised you all got her to confess."

"Well, we made her a deal that she'd have to have been stupid not to take," I replied.

"I know all about it," Abel spoke with a chuckle. "What's the catch?" he asked.

"She's not giving up her partner, but we know it's not Michael. I just wanted to run it by you before I went to clear him."

"Well, we got a confession from Linda; it's a start," he admitted. "Go on and cut Michael loose."

"Thanks," I spoke before leaving his office.

I walked downstairs and spoke to the guard.

"I need Michael Wilson," I spoke as I showed him my badge. "He's been cleared and we have to process him out."

"Wait here," the guard spoke as he confirmed the information with Abel.

He allowed me to enter the back and I walked to Michael's cell.

"Michael Wilson," I spoke aloud and he walked to the front.

The guard unlocked the cell and pulled the door open.

"Let's go," I spoke to him.

I saw a slight smile grow across Michael's face.

"I'm processing you out, and then you'll be free to go."

"Thank you," he spoke.

"I'm a fair guy," I added. "I don't believe in making anyone pay for something that they didn't do… and your alibi checks out."

Michael and I continued to walk towards the front.

"But, I do have a question for you, Michael," I mentioned as we walked. "Why would you go through all that you've been through if you know you were innocent?" I asked him.

Michael's smile left his face and he looked as though he were in deep thought.

"Julie's my cousin," he finally spoke. "Family comes before everything… but when it came to a point that I realized that she would pin the entire thing on me, I knew it was time to claim my innocence and get out."

"Us cutting you free is because we have no reason to hold you, Mike," I spoke as we reached the front desk. "This opens the door to plenty of other questions we still have, so don't leave town. Just know that you've been cleared of the charges for the robbery," I remembered so many questionable events leading to their arrest.

"Trust me, I don't plan on coming back to this place," Michael laughed as Isabella passed him a plastic bag with his things.

He signed a piece of paper and walked to the exit.

"Think he'll be back," Isabella whispered to me.

"Michael's a pretty smart guy. He'll stay off of our radar," I chuckled. "I gotta get back in here to Linda," I spoke as I walked off.

I re-entered the room and Jared stood across from Linda and Lisa.

"We all set?" I asked.

Linda nodded her head yes.

"We're good here, Detective," Lisa spoke.

"Let's go, Linda," Jared spoke.

I grabbed her confession from the table as Jared escorted her from the room.

"What made you come back?" I asked Lisa as Jared and Linda disappeared into the basement.

"I'm here to serve. If I have a client that needs help and they call me, I'm there for them," she spoke.

"Even if they did the crime…" I added.

"Can I be honest with you, Detective?" she asked.

I nodded my head.

"One real reason I pushed for a confession, is because of her most recent 'felony evading' charge. Why would she run from you?"

"In my time of being a law enforcer, I've learned that 99 percent of people run when they're guilty about something," I spoke.

Lisa sighed.

"Don't worry. We'll take care of her. Hey, it's safer for her to be in here rather than out on the streets," I admitted.

"Yeah, I hope you're right. I think I'm just going to remain in the area for a little while," she spoke. "Julie and I are supposed to be meeting in a little bit."

"That's interesting," we walked to the front. "We were going to talk to her again about the robbery... and since she's lawyered up," I began, "you have to be there," I chuckled.

Lisa laughed.

"Yeah, you're right," she replied.

"So, I guess we'll be seeing you shortly," I chuckled. "Maybe within the next hour or so," I explained.

"I'm just going to run over to the store for a moment."

"Well, we're going to question her again in about an hour-and-a-half," I spoke to Lisa.

"I'll be back," she walked out of the building.

I walked to the back towards Abel's office.

"One down, hopefully, just one more to go," I spoke to him.

"Trying to be top cop again?" Abel chuckled.

"Just doing my job," I joked. "Lisa's coming back in about an hour."

"Okay, perfect. You and Jared take a lunch. When you all get back, she should be here."

"You sure?" I asked.

"Positive. I'm assuming she's coming back for Julie, right?" he asked.

"Yeah."

"Yeah, you all need to take a break. Julie's gonna give you all everything she's got."

"Abel, we got this," I spoke as I left his office.

I walked to the front desk, where Jared resided as he spoke to Isabella.

"I'd hate to break up y'all parade," I laughed and clapped my hands together to get their attention, "but Abel told us to take our black asses on lunch."

"Yeah? That's what he said, huh?" Jared asked sarcastically.

I reached into my pocket and pulled out my debit card.

I chuckled, "Lisa's coming back to talk to Julie in about an hour, and he wants us to be ready to push a confession out of her."

"Shit, bro," Jared stood erect. "We don't need no damn prep. We got this."

"Yeah... but he's the boss man, so let's just do it," I joked. "Care to join us, Isabella?" I extended the invitation.

"I would," she started, "but I have a few things to finish here. "Maybe I'll catch up with you all."

"Sounds good," I pulled out my phone after I felt a vibration.

I received a text from Madison.

Jared and I walked towards the exit.

"Nope," Jared spoke as he took my phone from me. "We gotta plan how this is gonna pan out with Julie."

He looked at my phone and saw Madison's name with a heart emoji next to it.

"No time for Madison right now," he spoke as he put my phone in his pocket.

Here I was, a grown man, being told that I couldn't use my phone to text my girlfriend.

"Yes, Father," I spoke sarcastically.

14

"I hear that my cousin is free," Julie started as she stared at me.

"Who? Michael?" I asked as though I didn't know who she was talking about.

"Nah, we're talking about Casper, the friendly ghost," Julie rolled her eyes.

I forced a laugh.

"We got a comedian, Jared," I mentioned to him. "We have no reason to hold people if they're innocent," I adjusted my facial expression.

"So, if that's the case, why am I here in this orange jumpsuit?" she asked as she scanned Jared's facial expression.

"My boy just told you that we don't hold people if they're *innocent*," he assured.

"Meaning, you got something on me," she replied with a chuckle.

"Miss Watkins, you may want to tell your client to be quiet. She has two ears and one mouth for a reason," I spoke to Lisa.

"Julie, hush," Lisa whispered.

Julie looked at Lisa with a confused look but remained quiet.

"Your girl, Linda," I began, "she gave you up," I lied.

Lisa knew I was lying about the Linda giving Julie up, and threw a look of disapproval my way.

I widened my eyes at her as if to say, 'I'm just doing my job'.

"You're lying," Julie chuckled.

"Alrighty then," I spoke. "I don't need to sit here and try to work something out with someone who doesn't want to listen," I began to rise to my feet.

"Julie, you're looking at a minimum of 25 years for the robbery alone," Jared spoke as I stood.

"Try harder," Julie didn't seem interested in any deal.

"You want me to run down the list?" I asked her as I got closer to her.

"Humor me," she immediately replied.

"Robbery, felony evading, demolition, conspiracy," I started.

"All of which you're *trying* to prove," Julie retaliated. "Try harder."

I slammed my hand on the desk and both Lisa and Julie were startled.

"Such aggression," Julie chuckled. "It's cute coming from you," she winked.

"I get the impression that you feel that this is a game," Jared responded.

"Oh, it's all a game," Julie started.

"Be quiet, Julie," Lisa spoke.

"If you didn't realize it by now, you all are dumber than I thought," Julie laughed.

I looked at Jared as though I felt a confession was about to come out.

"Julie, that's enough," Lisa pleaded.

"No, Lisa," she laughed. "They need to hear this. You all are spending so much time focusing on pinning this robbery on me, yet you all just let Michael go and you all swore up and down he was my accomplice. Now you're saying it's Linda?" Julie shook her head as she chuckled. "God, the Chicago police are some reaching bastards."

"Reaching?" I chuckled. "Okay. We have your footprints at the crime scene. A freaking witness places you there, and you've been given up

"So *you* say."

"So evidence says," I corrected her.

I could tell that Jared and Lisa were both feeling a little uncomfortable. Julie and I were going back and forth, faster than the mind could process it.

"Detective," Lisa interjected, "why are we here?" she asked.

"We're trying to cut her a deal, but it doesn't seem to me like your client is interested."

"Julie, all of the evidence points to you. Linda's already confessed, so if we get a statement and a written confession from you, this saves both of us time in going to court and getting a much harsher sentence being thrown at you."

"Would you mind listing out her charges and potential time for each charge?" Lisa asked.

"Armed robbery," I spoke. "That's going to give her about 25 years alone if it goes to court. We're not even including the felony evading, the arson and demolition, conspiracy, and bribery of law enforcement," I was referring to her working with Linda.

"How much time would she be looking at if this were taken to court?"

"Jared, help me out here," I brought him into the conversation.

"What's that, 25 years for robbery, throw in an additional 5 for felony evading, ten for arson & demolition, and five more for the bribery and conspiracy charges... each," Jared spoke.

"Put it like this, if this goes to court and Julie is found guilty, your children will have children by the time you get out."

Julie was silent and stared at me; almost as though she could call my bluff.

"What are you all offering?" Lisa spoke.

"If Julie confesses the crimes, we'll knock the arson and demolition charges down to 3rd-degree charges, and we'll make the conspiracy charge vanish. We'll knock her 40-year sentence down to fifteen, with the possibility of parole within 7 years."

"That's a hell of a deal," Jared suggested that they take it.

"This is the problem with the police," Julie spoke. "I love how they try to pin all these charges on me, and then, they want to 'be my friend' and 'help me out'. All the damn empty threats," she cleared her throat, "they don't mean shit."

"This offer's only good for the next 24 hours," I spoke as I became annoyed with Julie.

"Either you take it, or you leave it," Jared added.

I rose from my chair.

"Come on, J, let's give them ten minutes to think it over, and if she needs longer, she can think about it overnight," I suggested as we exited the room.

"She's not budging," Jared told me as the door closed.

"Just like we predicted," I admitted. "But that's her life."

"So, we can't trip over it," Jared finished my thought.

"Precisely. Let them think over it, and hopefully, she takes the deal."

"And if she doesn't, oh well," Jared spoke.

***

Jared and I entered the room the next day; Julie and Lisa were already seated.

"Good morning, good morning," I spoke as I set the cup holder down. "I got you ladies coffee; I don't know how you all take it."

Jared sat the bag with the packets of cream and sugar down. "How are you all doing today?" Jared asked.

"Pretty well, Detective," Lisa spoke. "How about yourselves?"

"Pretty well. Have you all given any thought to what we discussed?" I asked.

"We have," Lisa spoke. She lightly tapped Julie.

"If I were to confess to this crime," Julie started nervously, "how would my record look?"

"The robbery charge wouldn't go away. It's here to stay," I spoke. "That is, if you're convicted or if you confess."

"You do have the opportunity to have the other charges wiped clear years after you serve your time. You'd have to talk to the DA or your PO about that," Jared added.

Julie looked at Lisa, and Lisa nodded her head.

"What's it going to be Julie?" I asked after moments of silence.

Julie thought for a moment and looked at the door. For a moment, I could have sworn she was going to run for the door.

Julie let out a slight chuckle.

"40 years doesn't do me justice."

"Yeah, well that's what's coming your way if you go to court and are convicted. Not to mention that all of the other deals are gone if you're found guilty," I added.

Julie grabbed one of the coffees and put cream and sugar in it before taking a sip.

"I got a confession for you," Julie spoke in a low tone.

"Here's my promise to you," Jared admitted. "Everything we've mentioned to you about the deal will be kept if you give us the verbal and written confession."

Julie shook her head.

"I planned the entire thing," she started. "Linda got me the blueprints of the bank, and everything took course from there."

"We're going to need more than that," I told Julie.

Julie let out a sigh.

"I approached Linda about a job. I knew the payout would be huge if we successfully pulled it off, so I figured, 'why not reach out to one of Chicago's finest to help pull this off', and I knew it would have had to be a White cop." Julie chuckled. "Not to mention that I went to school with Linda, so I knew her."

I looked at Jared and then back at Julie.

"So, we went to the bank the day before the robbery, and we disabled the security systems and the camera. We even went to that store to create an alibi," she took another sip of the coffee.

I shook my head in disgust.

"Julie," Jared began, "did Michael have any involvement in this robbery?"

"No," she spoke. "He knew nothing of it until all was said and done."

I had to excuse myself from the room.

We'd spent so much time trying to get Michael to come clean, when in reality, he knew nothing about the crime. And that fact that Julie allowed us to pursue her cousin, was overwhelming to me.

"Excuse me, ladies," I rose to my feet as I exited the room.

Abel waited outside of the room and greeted me as I exited.

"You got a confession," he started, "you should be excited."

"I should be," I admitted, "but I just think about all of the time wasted on trying to catch Julie. We wasted so much time trying to get Michael, and he was innocent all along."

"That's the police life. Sometimes, we make bad calls. We were 50% correct all along," Abel spoke.

"I know that sometimes we get bad calls, but it's a little bothering when you invest so much time, and both parties let you believe that."

"Yeah, but you can't control how others act. That's just the reality of this line of work." Abel finished.

Jared walked out of the room with handcuffs on Julie.

"The important thing is, you got her," Abel continued as he saw Jared. "It's time to get your head in the game. It's showtime."

"I guess the game's over, Julie," I spoke in a low tone as I watched Jared escort her away.

∎∎∎

Later that evening, as I arrived home, Madison greeted me at the door.

"Damn, girl," I spoke. "Almost got shot coming out of my home like that," I chuckled as I closed my car door.

"I'm sorry, baby," she chuckled as I stood in front of her.

She wrapped her arms around my neck and kissed me.

I put my hands on her slim waist and hugged her.

"How was work?" she asked.

"We closed the case," I spoke with relief. "We got a confession from both Julie and Linda. 15 years for Julie and seven for Linda."

"Congratulations," she spoke as she gave me another quick kiss on the lips. "So, what about that 2 million that they made off with?"

"We gave the account number and codes to the bank, so they're retrieving it back. I can only imagine how happy those customers must be."

"Yeah, if they don't switch banks," Madison spoke. "I know if it was me and I had a bank account with a small bank like that, and they got robbed, I would switch banks."

"You got a point," I admitted. "But that's their choice," I shrugged my shoulders slightly. "We did our police work in getting them their money back, so the rest is up to the bank and the customer."

"I've been thinking about you all day," Madison stated, switching subjects.

"Have you really?" I asked as I kissed her lips.

"Very much so," she looked into my eyes as if she could see my soul.

I looked at her slim figure, yet curvy in all the right places.

"Why don't you take a moment to show me how much?" I chuckled.

"Don't get nasty," she laughed. "Come on, I made you dinner," she spoke as we walked in the house and closed the door.